The Preacher's Son
Marc Adams

Leave a light.
Marc Adams

WINDOW BOOKS

You may contact the author, Marc Adams, via email at
marc@meetmarcadams.com
www.meetmarcadams.com
www.heartstrong.org

This is a nonfiction book.
To protect anonymity,
some names have been changed and
some situations differ slightly
from original occurrences.

ISBN Number 1-889829-00-5

Published in the United States of America.
Set in Times New Roman
Cover Design by Brainstorm Design and Marketing

for those who have climbed the hill...

1

The sky was so blue and the clouds so white it almost felt as if I was already in heaven. The wind on my face and the grass around me gave me courage. For the first time in a month, I smiled. I wished the task ahead of me would be as easily completed as climbing the hill. The burden of life had become so heavy.

I stretched out on the grass and looked at the sky, wondering which cloud would take me to heaven.

"Oh God," I said aloud. "I've been here before, so you know why I'm here now. There is so much pain inside and no one to help me with it. I just need it to be over. I can't do any more of the things I have to do now. Forgive me for making my life short and if I'm not going to be able to do something you wanted me to do."

Tears ran out of my eyes and onto the grass under my head.

"Why won't you just do this for me so I won't have to do it myself!" I cried out, feeling the same anger and loneliness I had felt every day of my life.

I didn't expect an audible answer, and I certainly didn't think God would end my life for me. That's why I had brought the razor blades to that quiet hill.

When there were no more tears to cry, a numbness settled over my body. I sat up and took one of the razor blades out of my shirt pocket. Ever so lightly, I ran the edge of the blade across my left wrist. This one, I thought to myself, would be for my failures. Switching hands, I ran the blade across my right wrist. This one would be for being gay.

I turned the blade at an angle and continued to scratch my right wrist until the skin turned white. This wrist, the one I had marked to bear the pain of my homo-sexuality, in and of itself, was enough for which to die. The cut I would make would deliver to me my freedom. There would be no more lies, no more ruined friendships, and no more shame.

The tears came again, and with them, a torrent of pain and anger. Those were the same emotions that shrouded my soul my entire life like a thick fog, muffling my happiness and ability to sustain peace.

No matter how much I wanted to, or how many times I ran the blade across my wrist, I could not bring myself to apply enough pressure to make me bleed. My desperation left me exhausted.

Defeated by my instinct to live, I laid in the field for another hour or so, letting my emotions heal and freeing my mind of the surge of negative thoughts that had brought me there. I believed then that God was there. Something always washed over my aching soul and healed me.

My father was the pastor of a small, independent Baptist church in Shavertown, Pennsylvania. My mother worked part-time as a nurse's aid at a hospital in the neighboring city of Wilkes-Barre. My four sisters and I spent our childhood and adolescent years there.

Shavertown and Wilkes-Barre were not exactly metropolitan melting pots. They were more like rural frying pans. Nothing much ever changed, because everyone liked everything the way it was. No one liked anything that challenged them or required them to make an alteration to the way they lived.

My parents adhered to the fundamentalist Baptist vein of Christianity. My father preached it in his church and he and my mother enforced it in our house — with a few modifications of their own.

Their belief was that their Bible contained the actual words of God. With a handful of a few embarrassing exceptions, they interpreted it literally as it appeared in the King James version. This strong belief affected every aspect of my life. It gave my parents freedom to do just about anything they desired under the guise that it was part of God's plan.

Part of this mandate from God included very physical punishments for anything done wrong. It was a convenient way to justify their emotions.

One of my first experiences of their disciplinary freedom happened when I was three years old. My father had carried me around some large street paving equipment parked near our house. My tiny hands managed to grab a slew of black grease off one of the trucks. Dissatisfied with how it felt, I wiped it on my chest and my father's shirt sleeve.

When my father noticed the mess I had made, he dropped me to the ground. Though I landed on my well-diapered butt, I will never forget the anger in his eyes as he jerked me to my feet and half-walked, half-dragged me back to the house.

It was that incident that raced back into my mind two years later when my father grabbed me by the ankles and began violently shaking me. I closed my eyes as the floor spun by three feet below my head.

"Put him down," my mother said. "I think he's learned his lesson."

"I don't ever want you to talk back to your mother again, do you hear me?" my father yelled.

He placed me upside down on a nearby chair.

I opened my eyes and looked at his face. I could see the anger burning in his eyes. As my body convulsed from fear, I watched them leave the room. I managed to turn myself around without vomiting. My ankles throbbed and I was too dizzy to stand.

It wasn't until I heard my parents bedroom door close that I cried. I wanted to scream but could only cry.

My older sister, Debbie, and younger sister, Carol, walked into the room and stood by my chair. Each of them had often been through similar dolor. Somehow, it was always easier for me to comfort them than it was for me to accept their condolences.

"Get out of here and leave me alone. I don't want you to stare at me!" I yelled, as my stomach churned.

They retreated as always. Alone, I was able to find a place for my pain. I was able to heal enough to continue.

"What happened to Marc?" Debbie asked the next morning at breakfast.

My mother glared at my father and pursed her lips in her usual "I'll-handle-this-one" manner.

"I think all of you need to understand that when we punish you, we're doing it because we love you. The Bible says, 'Spare the rod, spoil the child.' We're not going to disobey what the Bible tells us to do. And Marc, you need to stop pretending like you're hurt. I would hope that the only pain you're feeling is for your sin."

I bit the inside of my lip until it bled. Tears spilled out of my eyes and fell onto the napkin in my lap.

Throughout breakfast, the pain in my bruised ankles reminded me of my sin. The chorus of the song, *Jesus Loves Me*, began playing in my mind. I hoped it was true.

My sister, Debbie, is three years older than I am. Carol is a year and a half younger. Mary and Joy are four and six years younger, respectively. My parents did have another son who was born after Debbie. He died shortly after birth due to a heart condition.

From the time my sisters and I could hold our own heads up, our parent's brand of fundamentalist Christianity surrounded us. As young children we seemed to spend more time sitting in the pews of my father's church than anywhere else. We attended two Sunday morning services, an evening service and a midweek service.

Our parents continuously confronted us with the fundamentalist Christian plan of salvation that, upon acceptance of it, would save us from spending an eternity burning in Hell when we died.

The stories we were read from the Bible about Hell and what it was like for those who went there, left us terrified. By age seven, I found myself so frightened that I could hardly sleep at night. I was afraid to close my eyes because I might wake up in Hell.

One Sunday night, after a particularly effective sermon by my father, I tossed in my bed, tense and nervous. As she usually did, my mother came into my room to turn off the lamp.

"I don't want to go to Hell," I blurted out into the darkness.

I waited for her reply. We were not to use the word Hell in any casual way and I feared she might think that I was being flippant. Instead, she sat on the bed next to me.

"Do you know how you can keep from having to go to...ah, down there?" she asked.

"No," I lied.

I knew what I needed to do. I just wanted to make sure that I had remembered all the steps for my salvation.

"You need to ask Jesus to forgive all your sins and decide that you'll live the way he wants you to live. Just like he tells us in the Bible. Do you want to do that?"

"I don't want to go to Hell," I repeated. "I'm afraid to go there."

"Do you know that Jesus loves you and that he actually was crucified on a cross? He died to pay the price for all the sins you've done."

"I know he loves me."

I needed someone to love me.

"Now, you're not doing this just so you can stay up later than your normal bedtime, are you?"

My hopes fell to the floor. I was afraid that she wouldn't help me. But she did. She made me repeat a prayer she made up and that was it. Believing what I had said in that prayer was my salvation from eternal damnation in Hell.

I expected to feel a great relief, but I felt nothing except accountability. As a born-again Christian, my obligation to follow biblical guidelines, as well as the rules my parents created themselves, intensified.

I really did want to live right. I hoped that I could find something worthwhile in a relationship with the God I couldn't see or hear--the one I had to believe was there and loved me. I felt that something or someone was there.

Being the preacher's son, I really didn't have too much of a choice. The incredible feeling of obligation to follow in line with my parents was with me all the time. Our family was to be the example to the rest of our world. I also hoped that my conversion would lead to improved relations with my parents.

So, I began my dive into fundamentalist Christianity. From that day on, I began reading my Bible and putting complete faith in everything other Christians taught me.

I listened more intently to everyone except my parents. I couldn't hear them talk one way in church and then return home and say or do something completely opposite.

In my parents house, we were to keep ourselves from being contaminated by the rest of the world. That meant depriving ourselves anything considered worldly.

As preacher's kids and as Christians, we were required to adhere to a strict set of requirements. My sisters were not allowed to wear pants or shorts. Knee-length skirts and dresses made up the majority of their wardrobe. Jeans and shorts were out of the question for me, as well. No one, including my mother, wore makeup or accessories.

We hardly ever used our black and white television. Viewing was restricted to specific shows; *Wild Kingdom*, *Little House on the Prairie*, *Grizzly Adams* and an occasional pre-screened episode of *The Waltons*. We had to turn the television off completely during commercial breaks in those shows. We were taught that commercials contained rock and roll music which was created by Satan. As a Christian family, we boycotted stores playing anything but instrumental music.

Our limited television viewing was narrowed further by our parents' censorship of each program. If someone appeared on a show in clothing contrary to our dress code, we turned the television off until that person was off the screen. The same rule applied to scenes involving physical contact between opposite sexes.

Approved programs that contained scenes inside a bar or of alcohol consumption resulted in a swift termination of television viewing.

Everything taught at home as being the Christian way of life was reinforced by our friends. We were only allowed to develop friendships with other kids whose parents were also fundamentalists. Their lives mirrored ours and sometimes were even more restricted. Considering what we read in the Bible and what our parents told us, we accepted our lives as normal. Questioning the authority of the Bible or the authority of our parents was rebellion. We were often reminded of how the Bible gave approval for parents to stone their rebellious children.

After accepting Jesus as my personal saviour from Hell, I was able to consider myself better than everyone else around me who had not done the same. It gave me a sense of belonging. In belonging to that group, I learned how easy it was to feel superior to everyone else in the world because I had done the right thing. Everything everyone else did had to be wrong because they were not born-again Christians.

2

I entered fourth grade at Westmoreland Elementary School when I was nine. I never thought that I would be able to learn so much in one short school year. It wasn't academic knowledge I learned. It was Stephen.

Very few of my friends from the previous year returned to the same homeroom. I quickly found a new friend in Stephen. There was a magnetism from the moment we first exchanged hellos. It was the first time I was able to make a friend without much effort.

Stephen and I shared many of the same interests. I had always been prone to creative expression and when I was hanging out with Stephen, I didn't feel like I needed to hide those expressions. Our interests were years ahead of the other students our age, so we kept to ourselves.

My parents only allowed us to have friends who came from fundamentalist families. Stephen was Catholic, so we could only see each other when at school.

He accepted me without me having to change anything about myself. When I was around other kids my age, I found myself becoming a chameleon. This was the first friendship where we could disagree and not disintegrate the intimacy we shared. We disagreed on our religious beliefs, which were a big part of our lives. Stephen's parents had entrenched his mind in Catholicism, which conflicted with a lot of my fundamentalist viewpoints.

I couldn't care less about how Stephen thought he was going to get to heaven. I was simply glad to have a true blue friend. I had been lonely for a long time. When I was around Stephen, the loneliness disappeared. There was a kinship I had never before experienced. Our teachers noticed what was happening, even though we didn't have a clue.

Stephen and I hoped to share the same homeroom again the following year. Between the fourth and fifth grades, the district moved students to a different campus. But, as fate would have it, Stephen and I found ourselves in the same homeroom again.

I mentioned it to my fourth grade teacher one day when I saw her, and she made the comment that it was strange, since we were not allowed to be in the same class. I couldn't figure out what that meant, but I certainly wanted to find out. I knew my mother would get the answer I needed.

I recalled how my mother strong-armed the school to excuse all of us from the physical education classes that taught square dancing. Any form of dancing or excessive body movement was forbidden.

"I saw Mrs. Rothrock today in school, and she said that Stephen and I shouldn't have been put in the same classroom this year. Why don't you think they want us to be friends?"

"I don't know. I'll call her tomorrow and find out."

My mother was waiting in the living room for me after school the next day.

"Have you ever kissed Stephen?" she asked.

"No, of course not."

I *had* wanted to kiss him several times.

"Well, Mrs. Rothrock felt that you and Stephen had been spending too much time together and that you started liking each other more than just friends. Have you ever held his hand?"

"No way!" I exploded.

I wanted to hold his hand, but I never found the courage to do it.

"They weren't sure what you two had done. It's okay for men and women to kiss and get married, but it can't happen between two men."

"You're not making any sense!" I yelled.

I stormed away and went to my bedroom. I wasn't about to admit to my mother that I had fantasized about Stephen and several other boys.

The next year, my parents enrolled my four sisters and me in a private, church-sponsored school. Without the possibility of after school visits, and with telephone calls forbidden, I knew I would never see Stephen again.

The loneliness returned to my life. I knew I must have committed some sort of sin, but I didn't understand what it was. My first best friend had been carefully removed from my life.

The private school was Dallas Christian School, located inside the Dallas Community Church. The school had about sixty students from kindergarten through senior high. After taking placement tests, I entered at their sixth grade level, right where I needed to be.

The school's curriculum was Accelerated Christian Education and was a self-teaching method of education. There were no classrooms, only self-explanatory lesson books called PACEs. There were twelve PACEs per subject, per grade level. A monitor checked on each student daily and assigned a certain number of pages to be completed each day.

After every tenth page or so, there were brief quizzes. At the end of each PACE there was a self-test, followed by a final test. The final tests were taken in a special testing area. Except for the final test, each student was required to go to a scoring key in the middle of the learning center and grade their own work. Errors were corrected and a signature from the monitor was required before continuing.

The students had a lot of responsibility placed on their shoulders. It was easy to look ahead in the score key and memorize the answers to any upcoming quizzes. That is how most students did it and my sisters and I caught on fast. I was careful, though.

Students caught cheating were quickly "spanked" with a huge, wooden boat oar. Female students got five firm wacks on their butts. Male students had to drop their pants and were hit on the backs of their thighs.

The rules at Dallas Christian School mirrored the rules we lived by at home. Guys dressed uniformly in solid colored dress shirts, ties and dress pants. Girls wore dresses or skirts with a hemline below the knee. Pantyhose or knee high socks were also required.

Guys had to have short haircuts — off the collar and above the ears. Facial hair was not allowed. Girls could not wear makeup and only simple jewelry was permitted.

Each morning began with roll call followed by prayer and Scripture reading. We read the same chapter of the Bible each day for an entire month. At the end of the month, every student had to recite the designated chapter from memory. Failure to do so could result in expulsion.

My sisters and I were used to having to memorize Bible verses. Our parents required it. Unfortunately, the passages to be memorized never coincided, so we were constantly memorizing. Following the prayer and Bible reading, students broke up into groups for more intimate prayers and devotions, much like the ones held by my parents each night.

Another school rule prohibited attendance at movies or viewing inappropriate television programming. Parents were expected to support the rules.

There was also required attendance at a weekly chapel service, which was pretty much the same thing as a church service. Along with the usual educational subjects, completion of Bible-oriented PACEs such as Old Testament Survey, New Testament Survey, studies of the life of Christ and others like them, was required.

I was intrigued that I could do my work at my own pace. The benefit of A.C.E. schools was that progressive students could move through more than one grade level in a school year. With that advantage, I could graduate early.

I made that my goal. It gave me six years instead of seven to get out of my parents' house. As much as I missed Stephen and other friends I had made while in public school, the potential of gaining my freedom a year early was worth the sacrifice.

Ironically, my sisters and I were affronted more often for being preacher's kids at the Christian school than when we attended public school. I would have presumed that anyone attending a Christian school would be there mostly because of their religious perspective. We learned quickly that half of the student body were rejects from the public school system. They were expelled students whose problems, their parents believed, could be solved by placing them in a highly structured environment.

The end result was drug use, underage drinking, teenage pregnancies and sexual promiscuity that exceeded anything I had witnessed in public school. On many occasions, administrators would look the other way when a problem was brought to their attention. They couldn't afford to lose the tuition money.

Two years after we started attending Dallas Christian School, the pastor of the church, John Brooks, suddenly packed his office up and left. He and his wife moved out of the parsonage and disappeared. We were told in a chapel service that he had simply decided that he no longer wanted to be pastor of that church.

Having been around churches my entire life, I knew the story couldn't be true. I knew his secretary pretty well, as she had been a substitute teacher in the public school system when I was in the second grade. She told me that she had noticed that the pastor received mail on a regular basis from Dr. Jerry Falwell's Old Time Gospel Hour television program, as well as the Moral Majority. I knew about Jerry Falwell. We were occasionally allowed to watch his program on Saturday mornings.

The deacon board of the church confronted Pastor Brooks about his affiliation with Jerry Falwell's ministry. He was fired immediately when he admitted giving money to both the Old Time Gospel Hour and the Moral Majority. That church, my father's, and many others, considered Jerry Falwell a liberal.

The attention given to Jerry Falwell during the little scandal made me interested in hearing more about what he had to say. I wondered what he was doing or saying differently about Christianity that made him such a bad person in everyone's eyes.

3

I hit the floor hard. I used my hands to help me skid to a stop just before ramming my head into the kitchen door. My head was spinning. I could taste blood. I quickly ran my tongue along my teeth to make sure they were all intact.

The inside of my cheek was bleeding profusely from a tear caused from my father slamming his hand into the side of my face. I had not even seen his arm move.

I could feel my sisters' eyes staring at my back. Clenching my jaw, I attempted to sit up.

"He's bleeding Daddy! You knocked his teeth out. What did you do?" Debbie screamed.

My father spun around quickly, raising a spatula over his head.

"He's not bleeding," he snarled. "He got what he deserved and you'll get yours if you don't be quiet and finish eating," he threatened. "Marc, get back up on your chair!"

What Debbie thought were teeth was just the food

I had in my mouth flying out at the impact of my father's hand. I could barely sit. Standing and going to my chair at the table seemed an impossibility.

I felt like crying but I didn't dare do it. My throat began to burn as I tried valiantly to hold back the flood of emotion inside.

I did make it back to my chair. I ate enough of the charred food on my plate to be excused from the table. I always found a way to keep it together until I was alone in my room. This time was a little different, a little more difficult. I hated Christmas.

My sisters and I also hated Sundays. Without fail, we would all be disciplined for something gone awry during the morning services.

One Sunday, my mother accused Debbie of a minor infraction that I knew *I* had committed. All afternoon, my mother made routine trips to Debbie's bedroom to beat her some more — all in an attempt to harvest a confession.

In spite of listening to Debbie's screams and continuous pleas of innocence, I couldn't bring myself to confess. I just sat on the floor, bit into a pillow and covered my ears — waiting for the inevitable.

The discipline began at about 1:30 p.m. At 4 p.m., Debbie finally confessed to a crime she didn't commit. Most of the time it was easier to stop fighting.

"It would have been much easier if you would have just told me the truth right away," my mother yelled.

I tried to comfort Debbie and for weeks I felt guilty for letting her take the fall. I just couldn't tell my mother I was the responsible party. I didn't feel I could take much more of what they were giving. I contemplated leaving home many times, but there was nowhere to go. I gradually learned I could take much more than I thought.

My mother usually worked the 3 p.m. to 11 p.m. shift at the hospital. We had a reprieve from her antics on the days she worked. But it was equally as challenging to avoid triggering my father's anger. As I nursed my own wounds in my bedroom, I often heard the familiar sound of my sisters attempting to outrun my enraged father.

It was too much for me to fight for them and myself. I would end up with twice as many aches in my body. My sister Carol, however, had no problem speaking her mind to him. I always admired her valiant efforts.

One evening, when I thought it seemed unusually calm outside my door, she knocked on my door and asked me to follow her. She led me to my parent's bedroom door which was closed and locked.

"Listen," she whispered.

I didn't have to get very close before I could hear. My father had taken Joy into his closet and was giving her a good beating.

"Why is he hitting her in the closet?" I asked, knowing it was unimportant what she had done to warrant the beating.

"I've been screaming and yelling at him so much whenever he gets started, that he decided to hide her away and hit her. I guess he thinks that I won't be able to bother him in there."

Carol's disposition suddenly changed and she began pounding on the door.

"Stop beating her!"

Almost immediately, we heard the familiar squeak of the floorboards moving as my father stepped out of the closet towards the door. Carol bolted for her room.

"Why don't you pick on someone your own size?" I yelled at the door.

I knew that saying the last words would spare Carol any repercussions this time. I fled to my room and locked the door. Trembling from anger and fright, I crouched in the farthest corner.

Ten seconds later, my father kicked in the door. Splinters of wood flew everywhere as the lock tore out of the door. He grabbed me by the shoulders and pushed me against the wall.

"What I do in my room is none of your business!"

He slapped my face so hard, my head turned and my cheekbone hit against the wall. I kept my mouth shut and he left me alone. Alone.

My father assumed the pastorate of Pilgrimage Baptist Church in Shavertown, in April of 1970.

The previous minister had adopted an orphaned native American child. One Sunday, the minister told the congregation that since God had led him to adopt the little boy, it was now their responsibility to pay for everything the child needed. This was to be in addition to his salary.

The majority of the two hundred member congregation didn't like that idea and took their membership elsewhere, leaving about twenty members. The minister then decided that he needed to become more involved with the American Indians. He resigned and became a missionary.

The number of members in the church declined even more over the first few years after my father assumed the pastorate. It got to the point where he had to take a job because the tithe from the membership no longer covered his salary. Fortunately, the church had a parsonage for the pastor and his family. The large five bedroom house had a two car garage which eventually was converted to a small chapel and the other church building was sold.

The church was so small at that point that only seven pews would fit in the chapel and those were more than enough. Two older women, who had been with the church since its inception thirty years earlier, kept attending and that was all. However, when their health failed and they became homebound, the chapel became completely empty of any real church members.

Nonetheless, my father and mother would get us up early every Sunday morning and walk us through the kitchen into the small chapel. We would have a full-scale church service, including a tithe collection. I felt so ridiculous walking up to my sisters with an offering plate and collecting a quarter from each of them—especially since they were the same quarters my mother had handed us before we entered the chapel.

My father and mother firmly believed that because they prayed for new church members and because we had a hideous red and white sign nailed to our front porch, that people would come to their services. Not once in twelve years did my father go out "visiting" to recruit new members. Yet every Sunday morning and every Sunday night we held our own little church services. Eventually, my parents gave in and we went to someone else's church service for the evening service. They held fast to playing church for the morning service.

My father was offered several pastorates in neighboring towns, but he never took advantage of the offers. Perhaps my parents became very comfortable living rent free in the parsonage and were used to their regular jobs. Closing Pilgrimage Baptist Church would be admitting failure.

My father went to Lancaster Bible College to become a preacher immediately after high school. He was unable to get any type of skilled job. He worked as a maintenance man for a nursing home for minimum wage, which was barely three dollars at the time. My mother made more money as a nurse's aide. Still, we lived below the poverty level.

At the time, I didn't understand very much about making money. I knew that there were rich people and poor people. I knew that we fell into the poor category. If I had been educated more about career options, I probably would have grown up with even more anger towards my parents for not working harder to make my way smooth.

My mother encouraged my sister Debbie and me to follow through with our musical abilities. A woman who used to attend my father's church agreed to give us piano lessons.

I was soon composing my own songs. There was something revealing about being able to express myself in the music I played. Many times after being disciplined, I would walk out to the chapel, sit at the piano and play the saddest tune I could find. It was cheap therapy, but it worked.

My mother also forced us to provide "special music" during the Sunday morning and evening services. As embarrassed as I was to stand in front of an empty church and sing a hymn to my giggling sisters, I always enjoyed expending the energy it took to sing.

Soon, our parents were carting us off to convalescent homes on Sunday afternoons and holidays to sing for the elderly and dying patients.

I hoped that the words I sang would provide encouragement to everyone listening. There was always so much pain and suffering. I saw in many of their eyes the same loneliness that I felt. Except for the one gentleman who always ate the roses we handed out, I felt a connection to them and their anguish.

I first heard about AIDS when I was fourteen, during a church service at Ebenezer Baptist Church in Plymouth, Pennsylvania. We were there for a special service featuring missionaries from some foreign country. Somewhere along the way, the minister became sidetracked.

"I was reading in the newspaper the other day about these homosexuals that are moving into our community to take away our children. These faggots will stop at nothing to see that their agenda is fulfilled," the preacher ranted.

"Homosexuals are nothing more than child molesters and sexual deviants. Hold on tight to your children, especially your little boys. If one of these fags gets a hold of your son, they will recruit him into the homosexual lifestyle so that they can consume all of their filthy desires.

"God says in the book of Leviticus that these perverts are an abomination unto him. You'd better believe He's gonna throw'em all in Hell after the judgment. It seems as if we may have some relief from these wicked men. God is moving his hand in judgment right now against them. There is a new disease which will strike every homosexual. This is God's way of getting rid of these vermin.

"We need to thank God that one day, because of this disease, we will not have to worry about our sons becoming entrapped in a destructive lifestyle. We just need to be careful as God's people. This disease can be contracted through handshakes, public toilet seats or even just breathing the same air as a homosexual. So the best thing is to just stay away from them."

I had never felt an inclination to molest children, and I wasn't sure of the definition of a sexual deviant. But I felt a deep ache inside my chest. I knew I must be a homosexual because of my attraction to men.

Debbie and several other kids at school had often called me a faggot. I didn't know what it meant until that Sunday. I wanted to tell the preacher to shut up because I knew he must be talking about me. I bowed my head so no one could see my eyes.

I didn't want to grow up to be a bad person. I certainly didn't want to die or cause other people to die. But after what I had heard, it seemed inevitable.

When I got home to my room, I fell on my bed and cried myself to sleep. There was no place to go and no one to talk to about it. For the first time in my life, I felt alienated from God. He had always seemed so close, but that night he was far, far away.

I woke up the next morning unable to rinse my brain of the fact that I was going to die and go to Hell because of something I couldn't remember making a decision to do. The longer I thought about it, the more I realized that I hadn't actually ever had sex with another man. I had only fantasized.

I needed to control myself from turning those fantasies into realities. Although I had very little interest in it, I decided to spend more time pursuing a relationship with a girl so that I might be normal. The possibility of survival lifted my spirit.

In addition, I would have to quit masturbating — it was obviously a time where my fantasies took over. According to my Bible, masturbation was a sin.

I forced myself to pursue one of the two girls I knew who was available for a relationship. I never got along very well with either one, but I guessed the problem was that the objects of my fantasies were boys. If nothing else, showing interest in a girl would make me appear normal to everyone around me.

Two weeks after that sermon, I was walking in the woods behind my parent's house when I spotted a large white garbage bag half buried in the dirt about twenty feet off the path. I thought it might have been someone's dead pet, but the closer I got, I could see that the contents were books or magazines.

Curiosity got the best of me and I tore open the side of the bag with a stick. Dozens of *Hustler*, *Playboy* and *Penthouse* magazines spilled out. I looked around anxiously, hoping no one else had seen my discovery. I scooped the entire plastic bag up in my arms and half-walked, half-ran back to my parent's house. I slipped in the back door, went through the church and up to my room without anyone noticing. Breathless, I spread my find out on the floor.

I knew about pornography but I never could have picked up a magazine at a store. I had heard Jerry Falwell talk about these magazines many times. My discovery seemed to be God's way of helping me with my homosexuality, even though I knew that pornography of any kind was sinful.

I rationalized my conscience away by thinking that finding sexual gratification with a *Playboy* magazine would be instrumental in changing my mind about what I found exciting.

Two weeks into my world o' porn, I realized that I wasn't stimulated by the pictures of women. I was only fantasizing about the men. When I tried to concentrate on the women only, I felt nothing but emptiness.

After completing a creative writing section in one of my English PACEs, the learning center supervisor complimented me on my writing. I had never taken much of an interest in writing until I realized that I could write about anything I was feeling. I began writing short stories and poetry. I began submitting stories to publishers of Sunday School curriculum.

The first story I submitted was published immediately and the small payment seemed like a million dollars to me.

My parents were mildly supportive of my writing and music interests. They found little value in anything that didn't contain the steps to converting others to Christianity. They felt I should only be playing and singing hymns and limiting my writing to sermons that I could use later when I became a preacher.

I had never thought very much about becoming anything but a preacher before I was fourteen. Every other vocation was scorned by my parents, mostly because they wanted all of their children to follow their leading. Their leadership abilities obviously had much to be desired. My writing and music showed me that there were things I could do myself that made me feel good.

As I got a little older, I managed to push the boundaries on some of my parent's rules. It took a while for me to dispel the guilt I felt when I would leave the television on during commercial breaks. I would also adjust the radio to stations that played pop and rock music.

In both situations, I was amazed how much I enjoyed watching and listening. As with all sins, I knew that the more I listened and watched, the easier it would get and the less guilty I would feel.

I was enthralled with the creativity in the commercials I saw on television and those I heard on the radio. It only took a small amount of watching and listening before my interest peaked. It was then that I decided I would pursue a career in advertising, television production or both.

I had to choose a private Christian college to attend. Very few offered degrees in advertising or any creative field.

Debbie was the only one who faithfully watched Jerry Falwell's Old Time Gospel Hour television program on Saturday mornings. It was just a replay of Dr. Falwell's

Sunday morning service at Thomas Road Baptist Church. Besides, my mother usually ended up turning the television off whenever he used the word abortion.

One Saturday, I was walking through the living room on my way outside, when I noticed Debbie sitting with her eyes glued to the screen.

"What's so interesting?" I asked.

"You should come in here and watch this."

I walked in and sat on the floor.

"Dr. Falwell is showing pictures of his college. He's had it since 1971 and it's got two thousand students. Look! They're showing it again."

For the next half hour, we were given a visual tour of Liberty Baptist College and Liberty Mountain, the chunk of land and mountain owned by Thomas Road Baptist Church. When Dr. Falwell went into the television production studios and talked about how many students they had studying television, radio and film, I was hooked. He proceeded to walk through the brand new journalism labs and advertising classrooms.

I was sold after the thirty-minute tour. He was so knowledgeable about what Liberty was offering its students. I could feel his pride. He knew he was offering education in areas that other Christian colleges wouldn't even consider.

"Before you got here, he was talking about his teacher's education program." Debbie broke into my trance.

"Did it look good to you?"

"Much better than anything else I've seen. And Liberty has a special scholarship that pays for your first year's tuition if you are the son or daughter of a preacher."

Liberty Baptist College couldn't have been more appealing. Up until that point, Debbie's options were extremely conservative schools. While Liberty Baptist College was conservative, Jerry Falwell was still considered a liberal by most fundamentalist Christians we knew.

Throughout the next year, I made it a point to watch every Old Time Gospel Hour program. There were always references to Liberty to hold my interest.

On one program, he announced a special guest would be providing music and would speak briefly. I had never even heard of Anita Bryant. But from Dr. Falwell's introduction, she seemed like a famous person so I kept watching. The members of Thomas Road Baptist Church gave her a standing ovation as she walked to the podium and sang, *"The Old Rugged Cross."*

"Militant homosexuals."

As soon as the words rolled off Anita's lips, my mother swooped into the room and turned off the television.

"A true Christian woman wouldn't talk about things like that," she bristled.

I had heard the words *gay* and *homosexual* before but never *militant* homosexual. In my mind, I pictured gay men with guns and other weapons. I had to find out what she was talking about.

The next morning I faked a headache so that I could stay home from church. I wanted to have a chance to hear what this woman had to say. The same Old Time Gospel Hour program was shown on another channel on Sunday mornings.

While the rest of my family played church

downstairs, I turned on the television in my parents bedroom and watched with more anticipation than I had ever felt for anything else.

"I have spent years trying to rid our neighborhoods and our schools of these vermin," Mrs. Bryant went on, after using that term again.

They started showing footage of gay men protesting with signs outside an auditorium where she was speaking.

"They want nothing more than to take our children and molest them. They want the opportunity to teach in our schools so that they can get even closer to our children. They need to keep their ranks up so they have to recruit children whenever they can."

There it was again. The inference that gay men were child molesters. I was anxious for the woman to get off the stage so I could hear if Dr. Falwell had an opinion to inject.

My dream of going to Liberty Baptist College began fading as a stream of hate spewed out of Dr. Falwell's mouth. How could I be around someone who had so much hate for people who had feelings just like mine?

"But you know what?" Dr. Falwell added, just as I was about to turn off the television. "I believe that it doesn't matter who you are or what your life is like. If you want to change, if you want a new life and spend an eternity with Jesus, He can change you."

I had only assumed I could change. I never heard anyone promise it.

"Jesus wants your heart and he wants your life," he continued. "It doesn't matter if you are a homosexual.

Jesus will change you. He'll give you a new life and a new mind. I have seen many men turn from their homosexuality. That's the power of Jesus Christ. Why don't you let him?"

I felt something on my chin and brushed at it. I was crying. Without realizing it, I had been broken by Dr. Falwell's invitation. No one had ever promised me that there was a way to avoid becoming a child molester and getting AIDS. In all my efforts to change, I must have missed something.

4

The first time I stepped onto the campus of Liberty Baptist College was in August of 1983. We were taking Debbie there to begin her freshman year.

I envied her. She got to go to this place, this haven, where our parents couldn't touch her. She got to choose when she wanted to talk to them. I knew the road through college would be hard for her since she had to make it on her own. But that type of challenge made my mouth water.

I made a promise to myself that I would put aside my depression and feelings of inadequacy and make my upcoming junior year my final year. If I set my mind to it, I could take advantage of the A.C.E. curriculum and graduate a year early. I'd only be sixteen when I entered college, but I was up to the challenge.

I returned to Pennsylvania with my mission firmly rooted in my soul. I shared my plans with Carol, who was very supportive. I knew she was disappointed because she didn't want to be left at home without me.

When school started two weeks later, I was still high off the anticipation of my freedom. I wanted to let the principal, Gloria Lange, know of my intentions. Successfully reaching my goal would make me the first student in the history of the school to take advantage of the accelerated learning benefit.

"I am eager to start," I told her, three days into the school year. "I'm looking forward to graduating early and then going to college."

"I don't think you can do it," she replied, not looking up from her *Better Homes & Gardens*.

"Of course I can. You sound like everyone else when I first started writing. Everyone said that I couldn't get published because I was so young. But I did it. Now, magazines are asking me to contribute articles and stories."

Gloria looked at me.

"It's a lot of work to graduate early. You may not be ready to take on some of it."

"I didn't come to your office today to get your permission. I came to talk about my goals as a student. I'll look for encouragement elsewhere," I said, as I left her office.

I really only needed God's help to get through that school year. It was just as well. When I graduated early and went off to college, I'd be on my own anyway.

Debbie encouraged me by sending copies of the campus newspaper, *The Liberty Champion*. Reading about Liberty kept me fueled as I plunged into my work.

I needed to complete 136 PACEs to have enough credits to graduate. Normally, it took three or more weeks to complete a PACE. I didn't have that kind of time.

I had to complete one PACE every other day to reach my goal.

I tried not to cheat by looking ahead in the score key. I didn't want to go to college unprepared.

I managed to squeak through physical education classes by only remembering to bring a change of clothes once a month. I was too busy to go out in the snow and play touch football with guys who bragged how they spent their weekends "chasing niggers and fags" out of their trailer parks.

The lecture Debbie had warned me about came shortly before Christmas.

"We know you're going to graduate this year, honey," my mother began, in the most insincere tone. "Your father and I have some things to talk about with you."

"We know you sent your application to Liberty and we know you want to study television and advertising," she continued. "But if you do go to Liberty College, you'll be doing it on your own."

"We really would like you to reconsider your choice of schools, as well as your major. A true Christian has no place working in a worldly environment like television or advertising. You should think about using your talents for the Lord. You have a beautiful singing voice and you can write. Why don't you do something that will bring glory and honor to God?"

"Will you at least take me there in the Fall?"

"Yes, we'll take you and Debbie there. That is, if she still wants to go back."

Leave it to my mother to call it Liberty College instead of Liberty Baptist College and also assume that

Debbie would come to some kind of realization that Jerry Falwell was a liberal.

It would cost me approximately $4,000 a year to attend Liberty. My first year's tuition was waived because I was a preacher's son. I received a state of Pennsylvania grant which covered my room and board. The only thing that remained unsettled was cash to pay for books, laundry and other small items. I planned to get a job that would help with those expenses.

My parents *graciously* agreed to advance me the $150 confirmation fee that was due once I was accepted. I had to use any money I received from graduation gifts as collateral. Everything was falling into place. That's how I knew it was the right thing to do. With that kind of reinforcement, I couldn't fail.

"I don't know how many times I'm going to have to tell you kids to turn off your lights when you leave your rooms!" my father ranted, as he came down the stairs.

My sisters and I had gathered in the living room for the daily session of Bible reading and prayer. I was sitting closest to the living room doorway, so my father focused his anger on me as he walked into the room.

"I'm telling you kids, your mother and I are going to start taking money out of your allowances if you don't start respecting things around here."

I couldn't keep silent.

"I've been in this family for sixteen years and I've never gotten an allowance. Besides, it would be your money anyway, so what difference does it make?"

My father had already walked past me but he turned

and swung his hand up against the side of my face. I felt his knuckle hit my jaw.

"Don't ever mouth off to me again!" he roared.

I rose to my feet, realizing for the first time that I was taller than him.

"Don't ever hit me again," I said calmly, as I stared into his cold eyes.

He swung his hand back and hit me on the same spot. I didn't flinch this time and I didn't cry. I clenched my jaw and prepared for another strike. He had to get a response to feel like he had accomplished something. I gave him nothing. He turned around and walked away. That was the last time my father hit me.

Graduation was held on a Sunday afternoon. There were only six graduates in my class. Each of us had to give a brief speech including our favorite Bible verse and a round of thank you's to our families.

As I surveyed the crowd of about three hundred people, I couldn't see anyone who had loved me enough to support me. No one I had invited to my day of glory showed up, except my parents and my sisters. The only person there for me was my escort to the after graduation party, Danielle Frye. I wasn't interested in her as a dating prospect, but graduates were required to bring someone of the opposite sex to the party.

For the first time in my life, I realized how different I was from everyone else in that auditorium. Most of them would live and die in that town. Four out of the six graduates were already engaged to be married.

I ad-libbed my speech because the one I prepared

was cocky and full of lies.

The party after the ceremonies was cut short when my father pulled me from a photo shoot for the local papers. He felt we should go home and get ready for church.

I sat in the back seat of the car and fumed for the thirty minute drive home. He managed to steal the morsel of recognition I was getting for my accomplishment.

"Marc, your father wants to talk to you out in the church," my mother announced.

My father was sitting alone on the front pew. I was very uncomfortable. Yet, I knew that this could be a turning point in our relationship. I wondered if he was going to give me money for school.

"Mom said you wanted to talk to me," I said, as I sat on the pew behind him.

He turned around. I looked up at him, longing to see something other than the anger and coldness I had seen every day of my life.

"In two days you'll be off to college," he began. "You'll be out of this house and out of our control. We will no longer have anything to do with how you live your life."

He paused and stuck his finger in my face.

"Someday you're going to fail. You'll think to yourself, 'Mom and Dad were right.' Then you'll come back."

He got up and walked out of the church. My heart beat wildly as I blinked back tears. I could still see his finger pointing at me even though he was gone. I looked at the Bible on the communion table ten feet in front of me. The words on its pages had often been a source of comfort. There was nothing in there that could comfort me that day.

5

I knew what I was in for when I checked in on registration day. The lifestyle rules at Liberty were strict, but far less rigid than those in my parent's home. All of the rules were published in a manual known as the Liberty Way. Upon arrival, each student signed a form which stated their agreement to every rule.

Everyone had to be in their dorm room by 10:00 p.m., Sunday through Thursday. All lights had to be out by 11:00 p.m.

On Tuesdays and Thursdays each dorm floor was split into multiple groups called prayer groups. Each group had a designated prayer leader, usually an upper class student. The meeting included the sharing of prayer requests, praying for those requests and a short Bible lesson. These meetings offset the Monday, Wednesday and Friday morning chapel services. Attendance was required of all students. Each student had to sign in and absentees were disciplined.

Students were also required to attend Thomas Road Baptist Church's Sunday school and Sunday morning services. Students were bussed to Thomas Road on school busses.

The Sunday evening service was held on campus in the multi-purpose center. A Wednesday evening prayer service was also held. Students could choose between the Thomas Road sanctuary or the on-campus service. Again, attendance was taken at every service.

Those requirements were very familiar to me. It was the relational rules I didn't understand. Dating for freshmen, sophomores and juniors was restricted to on-campus activities only. No public displays of affection between members of the opposite sex were allowed. That rule included hand-holding, kissing, hugging, etc.

Since only seniors were permitted to have cars, it was difficult to circumvent the rule. (Wheel locks were placed on vehicles owned by underclass students who drove to school. The locks were removed only when the student was returning home for a weekend or holiday break.) Every student was required to have pre-approved, written permission from the dean's office to go home or anywhere else for the weekend.

Students were required to live on campus unless they had senior status or were over the age of twenty-two. The campus had twenty-three tri-level dormitories. The average dorm floor held eighty students with three or four per room. No microwaves or televisions were permitted. Television had to be viewed in one of three television lounges.

Only pre-approved Christian radio stations could be played. Contemporary Christian music or Christian rock was not allowed. Music by artists like Amy Grant was contraband. (Even though at that time she had not experienced any crossover success.) It was the style of music rather than the lyrics that was offensive. Possession of music by a secular music group or an unapproved Christian group always resulted in write-ups and confiscation of the offending cassette, album or compact disc.

Each floor had two upper-class student resident assistants called RAs. It was their responsibility to enforce all rules of behavior as stated in the Liberty Way.

They would check each room before all required church services. They were also responsible for writing up anyone whose room didn't pass morning clean-up inspection. Beds had to be made, the floor vacuumed, the sink cleaned, and trash cans emptied.

During these room checks, RAs would rummage through closets, dressers and other personal areas to check for illegal music or reading material. RAs would also stake out Lynchburg hangouts to ensure that no one except for seniors was having an off-campus date. The television lounges were also monitored by RAs. Television programs had to be pre-approved.

Attendance at movie theaters was forbidden, regardless of the film or the rating. RAs would hang out at exits and scour the theater parking lots looking for Liberty Baptist College parking permits on cars. Anyone attending a movie was issued a write-up. The RA's tuition was waived in exchange for their efforts.

After a student received a specific number of write-ups, the student was charged a fine which had to be paid or the student would be expelled. The fine could range from five bucks to hundreds of dollars. The Liberty Way was unclear how the school spent the money.

Liberty's dress code was not unlike my high school. Male students had to wear ties, dress shirts and pants. Female students wore dresses or skirts. Pantyhose was required at all times unless knee high socks were worn. Jeans were only permitted after class hours and during the evening meal at the college cafeteria, Saga.

All of the rules considered, I signed on the dotted line enthusiastically. I had made it! This was my freedom. There were things offered to me at Liberty that couldn't be found anywhere else. I was finally out of my parent's vise-like grip. I was moving in the direction of my goals and I was part of the fastest growing Christian college in America. I was finally part of something that was vibrant instead of dying.

No tears were shed when my family left. My mother, Mary, Carol and Joy hugged me good-bye, while my father waited in the car. I didn't care.

I returned to my dorm and spent some time getting to know the two RAs for my dorm floor, Brad and Scott. Scott was kind of cold and withdrawn, but Brad was a gentle guy who covered his vulnerability by exuding a tough guy image.

As I walked around and met the guys in my dorm, I realized I was evaluating whether or not I experienced a physical attraction to them. Brad was one of the people who immediately made my blood boil.

I had never met so many guys who were interested

in getting to know me. As I got to know them, I realized that just about everyone there was reared in situations similar to mine. All of us had been captured by Jerry Falwell's charisma and saw through him, our own personal opportunity to find more for our lives. All of a sudden, I didn't feel so alone.

I had to suppress myself whenever Brad was around. I explained away the attention he was paying me as only friendliness. It was Liberty Baptist College— there couldn't be any homosexuals in attendance. My acceptance into the institution was a fluke.

After a few weeks of becoming accustomed to my new life and my class schedule, I set out to get a part-time job. I looked through the classified ads in *The Liberty Champion*, the school newspaper. The only interesting position was for a layout assistant for the college yearbook. There was some scholarship money offered so I sent a letter of interest.

I didn't expect to get a response in two days. I was in my dorm room when I was startled out of studying by a knock on the door.

"The door's open. Come in!"

A tall, blond-haired guy walked into the room. My throat went dry and for the first time in my life, I was paralyzed by a burning sensation that shot through my body.

"I'm looking for Marc Adams. He responded to my ad in *The Liberty Champion* for an assistant in the yearbook office."

"That's me."

I slid off my bunk bed and walked over to him. I was suddenly very self conscious of my appearance.

"My name's Todd Tuttle."

"Oh yeah, we're in the same physical education class. I remember hearing the instructor call your name the other day. You've got a lot of T's in it."

I was rambling and I knew it. I had to avoid throwing myself at him.

"I've got some writing samples here as well as a copy of my high school yearbook. These should help you."

I watched carefully as Todd flipped through the samples. He didn't seem to be paying much attention to what was in front of him. It made me nervous to think maybe he felt uncomfortable standing so close to me. I stepped back. He looked at me and smiled.

"Why don't we go next door to the yearbook office? I want to show the editor these samples."

I would have followed him to China, but I managed to find contentment in going only to the yearbook office. That night, I officially became a member of the Liberty Baptist College yearbook staff.

Todd was the layout editor and explained how we would be working very closely together to design the pages and choose the photographs for the book. He was seventeen, a sophomore and a pastoral major. He was at Liberty to become a Baptist minister. I was confused by his career choice as I eyed his cartoons and illustrations hanging around the office.

I tossed and turned in my bed for hours that night. Todd seemed like a great guy to work with and have as a friend. I didn't want to screw up a working relationship and possibly a friendship over the dark passions that brewed inside me. I fell asleep that night asking God to forgive me for my lustful feelings. I knew that I had to start pursuing a heterosexual relationship before Satan got the best of me.

My schedule of classes at Liberty during my first semester was fairly easy. There were some required courses like history, math and two Bible study classes. I excelled in my first television production class. The professor, Dr. Judy Saxton, was also my academic advisor. She was the first woman to earn a doctorate in her field. She knew how to convey boring television history facts in an understandable and easily recalled manner.

The two Bible study classes were a bore. I had just been through a survey of the Old and New Testaments in high school. Nothing had changed. There were no new points of view. Besides, my parents had made sure that I was a whiz at that stuff. My Old Testament Survey class was at 8:00 a.m. Monday, Wednesday and Friday. I dozed, as Dr. Williams attempted to dazzle us.

One morning, while waiting for class to begin, someone sat down next to me conveniently spreading his legs a little so that one of them touched mine.

"How are you?"

I hadn't even had a chance to look up but I recognized Todd's voice. I smiled at him.

"I'm doing fine. I didn't know you were in this class."

"Well, I usually arrive late so I sit in the back. I can't believe you pull yourself out of bed and get here early."

"I figure the sooner I get here, the sooner it will be over."

"You probably got most of this by going to that Christian high school, didn't you?"

I rolled my eyes and nodded. At that moment, Dr. Williams walked up to the podium and opened the class with the usual prayer.

We were supposed to close our eyes, but I couldn't help keeping mine open to look at Todd. There was something so gentle about him. I suddenly got the urge to reach over and lay my hand on top of his. Dr. Williams ended his prayer and brought everyone back to consciousness before I could do it.

I knew that if I would have touched Todd's hand I would have had to pay a price. Not only would he know I had homosexual feelings, he would have to report the incident to the dean's office. That class seemed to last forever. I just wanted to get away from him.

"Have you eaten breakfast yet?" he asked, after the lecture.

"No. I planned to go before my next class."

"Let's go together," he invited. "I'm starved."

"For Saga's famous green eggs and ham?"

"You've noticed it, too? What do you think that is?"

"We probably don't want to know. We should just eat it and not ask too many questions."

Todd laughed and punched my shoulder. I was caught off guard and almost fell over. Didn't he know he couldn't touch me?

We opted for color correct breakfasts. Todd's

choice of Captain Crunch and my choice of corn flakes showed some initial differences.

"You said the other night that your father was a preacher."

"He used to be more of one than he is now," I replied. "His church is very small. In fact, now, there are almost no members."

"Was it weird growing up as the preacher's son?"

"It's all I knew. But you know, my sisters and I all went to private Christian schools for the most part. Everyone had some reason to be there. There were always so many unattainable expectations for me. I hated it."

"That's awful. I don't think I could have gone to a Christian school. I was always too active in extra-curricular activities."

"Like what?"

"I played soccer, did theater, art stuff — you know, the usual."

I didn't know.

"I played soccer for my high school. There was a league for the Christian schools. We just didn't play any public schools or Christian schools based out of churches that believed differently than our own."

"That's stupid."

"Tell me about it. The real rivalry and competition was between schools who never got to play against each other."

Todd laughed.

"That would have killed me. I told you I'm a goalie for the Liberty soccer team, didn't I?"

That explained the legs.

"No, you didn't. That's pretty cool. When's your

next home game?"

"Thursday. Why don't you come? I can always use the support."

"I'll be there," I promised.

The more time we spent together, the more I was able to open up to Todd. He was the most inquisitive person I had ever met. He knew how to make me feel comfortable enough to open up and let him inside.

"Have you ever looked at dirty magazines?" he asked suddenly, one day.

"No."

I was so surprised by the question, I couldn't help lying. Until then, my impression of Todd was that he truly lived his Christianity. I wouldn't have expected him to bring up such a topic. I looked around the office to make sure that we were the only people there.

"Actually, I have."

I couldn't believe my confession.

"About two years ago, when I was fourteen, I found a stash of magazines in the woods behind my parent's house. I knew looking at them was wrong. It was hard for me to throw them away."

"My dad kept lots of magazines in the house," Todd admitted. "I got to see whatever I wanted. And you're right, it is difficult to put them away."

"I was addicted in five minutes," I continued my confession. "But that's behind me now. I spent a lot of time praying about it and God really helped me through it."

As we got ready to leave for the night, I stood up and leaned forward against the drafting table so that he could walk past me. He stopped directly behind me. He didn't touch me but he was so close I could feel his body heat and his breath on the back of my neck.

"Stay away from those magazines," he whispered into my ear.

He turned his head and smiled at me once again before walking out the door.

I couldn't tell if he was making a joke, making fun of me or trying to turn me on. He was doing an excellent job of turning me on, but I had to believe that he was joking. I couldn't accept that someone as good of a Christian as Todd could have homosexual feelings. The intensity of my attraction to him was beginning to get the best of me. I thought I was falling to my knees because I was weak with passion.

"Oh God, I don't want to screw up this friendship!" I prayed. "Why don't you just take these awful feelings out of me! How can I go on if this is all I ever feel?"

6

I was late for chapel the next morning and I avoided sitting with Todd and his roommate, Ron. But I could see them from where I sat. I still felt dead inside. I was unable to determine if God had answered my prayer.

My classes went by in a blur. I felt detached from everything and everyone. After dinner, I went to the yearbook office and started to work on the new set of pages our office assistant, Sheila, had given me. Todd wasn't there when I arrived. I didn't care. I couldn't.

"Marc, your sister Debbie is outside and she wants to talk to you," Sheila said, after I had been there for an hour.

Todd walked in as I was walking out.

"Thanks," I mumbled to Sheila, as I breezed by him. Just before walking out, I turned around and looked. He was smiling at me.

Debbie was standing outside shivering. Her blouse was covered with blood.

"God, Debbie, what happened!"

The words barely got out of my mouth before she threw her arms around me and began crying. I pulled her arms from around my neck so I could look at her.

"Tell me what happened. What's all this blood?"

She wiped her eyes and leaned up against the building.

"I met this guy who works at Saga. His name is Wesley and he asked me out tonight. We went out to eat and then went to his apartment. All of a sudden, his ex-girlfriend showed up and started banging on the door."

She paused and started to cry.

"Wesley told me to go hide in his bedroom and not to come out until he knocked on the door. He let his ex-girlfriend in and she had a knife. She tried to stab him. He grabbed the knife by the blade and tried to get it away from her. She almost cut his thumb off."

"Is he okay?"

"He had to go to the hospital and get stitches. Sixty stitches all the way around." She circled her thumb with her index finger to show the location of the wound.

"I called the cops and they're out looking for her."

"This guy works at Saga? Sounds like he needs to get a better class of friends. Are you okay?"

"I'm okay. Just frightened. I never expected something like this to happen. He doesn't go to school here, he just works here."

"That explains why he has his own apartment and car."

"He's so nice, Marc. I really like him a lot."

"Yeah, but Debbie, you just can't go off with some guy you hardly know! You could have really been hurt!"

"Please don't be upset, Marc. I came to you

because I needed to talk to someone."

"I'm sorry."

I embraced her and we talked for a few more minutes before she felt calm enough to leave.

When I walked back into the yearbook office, the smile had disappeared from Todd's face.

"Is everything okay?" he asked.

"Sure. Debbie just hooked up with some guy with a wacko ex-girlfriend who tried to kill him."

"What?"

"Don't worry about it, it'll be fine.   It's her problem. I don't know what she thought I could do to help her."

It was one of those rare, seventy degree November days when I next saw Debbie. She had called and left a message with my roommates for me to meet her outside Saga.

While I preferred to exit the campus early on Saturdays, I made this exception because we had not seen each other in several weeks. She had started baby-sitting on the weekends for a woman she had met at Saga.

"It's almost like summer, isn't it?" she asked, as she sat on the bench next to me.

"It's beautiful. It's a shame that in a week it'll be forty below zero and snowing."

"I need to tell you something."

Dread crept up inside my chest. What would it be now?

"I've been sick for about a week now. I went to a doctor and he told me I'm pregnant."

I closed my eyes. My world was changing again. "What? How?"

"Wesley's the father."

"Well, what are you going to do?"

"I'm not too far along. I should be able to finish this semester without anyone noticing."

"What are you going to do then? Go home?"

"No, I'll move in with Wesley."

"So, you'll quit school and get married?"

She sighed and shifted nervously.

"I don't think we'll get married. Maybe once the baby is born I'll come back to school. Wesley's black," she blurted.

I wasn't surprised. She had dated several other black guys.

"I don't care if he's green. If the dean's office finds out, they certainly will care."

"You're not going to turn me in, are you?"

The thought *had* crossed my mind.

"Of course not. I'm here if you need me. I would like to meet Wesley, though. He's a part of your life, so I'd like to get to know him."

"Okay. No one at work knows except for Lori, the girl I baby-sit for."

"Any other news I should know?"

"Just one last thing," she smirked. "I'm not going home for Thanksgiving. I'm going to stay here at Wesley's apartment. I can't stand the thought of being around Mom and Dad."

"So are you really baby-sitting for Lori?"

Debbie smiled coyly and shook her head.

"You're too smart for your own good. Sometimes

I baby-sit for her, but mostly she just lies for me so that I can spend the weekend with Wesley. She signs the paperwork I have to turn in saying that I will be off campus for the weekend."

"Aren't you afraid you might get caught?"

"No. People do it all the time. They never check."

Everything was hazy after that point. I couldn't comprehend how Debbie would take such risks when it was actually a privilege to be at Liberty, instead of at home with Mom and Dad. She was really blowing it and that made me mad. I couldn't reprimand her, though. I wanted to remain her friend.

The memory of her standing outside the yearbook office door in a bloody blouse was fresh in my mind. I didn't trust Wesley at all, even though I had never met him. He seemed to have changed Debbie's life. She didn't seem happy anymore, just tired and anxious. I could tell that as much as she had told me, she was still hiding a lot.

I battled the urge to go to the dean's office. I rationalized away my responsibility by remembering that she was responsible for her decisions. God would take care of the rest. I crossed a line by not turning her in, but keeping her trust and being loyal to her was more important. I could have been expelled for withholding such information.

I tried to put Debbie and her personal problems out of my mind that weekend. I had tests in many of my classes the following week so I found a quiet corner in the library and buried myself in studying. By Monday, I was ready to go for it and get the final week before Thanksgiving out of the way.

As I was walking into chapel on Monday morning,

Linda, Debbie's roommate, stopped me.

"Marc, I need to talk to you."

We sat on a bench outside the auditorium.

"Debbie went to Lori's house to baby-sit this weekend and she didn't come back. She usually comes back to campus on Sunday night. She hasn't called or anything."

I knew it would come down to something like that. I just didn't expect it to have happened so quickly.

"To start, Linda, Debbie hasn't been baby-sitting for Lori on weekends. That's just been an excuse. She's been staying over at her new boyfriend Wesley's apartment."

Linda didn't seem surprised.

"Well, Marc, there's something you should know about Wesley. He's never been a student at Liberty. He's not even a Christian. He's an ex-convict on parole for assault and theft."

"What? Why is he working in Saga?"

Linda shrugged her shoulders.

"I don't know. I only know about this because my boyfriend, Steve, is a shift manager there. Many of the employees come from outside the college, and many of them are ex-convicts on parole."

"Well, that doesn't mean that Wesley's still a criminal."

"Steve fired him yesterday because they suspected him of stealing silverware."

I laughed.

"This is going to be a great day, I can tell already."

"I think we should go to the dean's office."

"I know," I agreed. "I have a test in my class after

chapel. After that, we can go. I'll meet you there in about an hour and a half."

I was pulled from my class in the middle of the exam and escorted to the dean's office. Dean Baker handled student situations like Debbie's. I was just grateful that *I* wasn't in trouble.

"We have been informed by your sister's RAs that she has quit school to move in with her boyfriend," he said, with the warmth of an iceberg.

"Debbie called them this morning and let them know. Why do you think she's doing this?"

"I don't have a clue."

"Your sister's roommate told us that you knew she was spending weekends with her boyfriend."

Linda had betrayed me. She had gone to the dean's office ahead of me.

"Debbie told me on Friday," I admitted.

"And why didn't you come forward immediately?" he asked, sternly. "We've been aware of your sister's activities for quite some time. I find it hard to believe that you just found out on Friday."

I knew what he was trying to do.

"First of all, I didn't know until Friday, so don't insinuate that I am lying to you. Second, there is a portion of the Liberty Way which is directed to parents. You've promised my parents that you will take care of their children. You're telling me that you've known for some time that Debbie was sleeping with Wesley and you did nothing about it?"

I knew it was all or nothing. I stood up and leaned on his desk.

"How dare you try to accuse me of not turning in

my sister! You are the responsible party here, not me! My parents trusted you. I refuse to sit here any longer and have you try to cover your mistake by shifting the blame to me. This is your problem!"

I turned around and walked to the door, stopping just before walking out. I turned my head around to look at him.

"I worked hard to come to this school. I love being here. I'm as much of a Christian as you are. I would never do anything that I didn't feel was right."

I walked out the door. I was afraid to stick around to hear his response. I brushed past his secretary and was about to exit the building when I heard him open his door.

"Why don't you come back into my office and talk about this some more?"

I could tell by the tone of his voice that his attitude had changed. I returned to his office.

"I am sorry that I tried to do that," he said nervously. "I understand that under the circumstances, you did the right thing. We don't want your parents to feel like we abused their trust."

He was concerned about publicity. I couldn't believe it. I decided to use the opportunity to exercise a little power.

"Are you aware that my sister's boyfriend is an ex-convict?"

"I know about the rehab program down there. We knew about Wesley's background."

7

I relayed the entire story to Todd that night. He responded by sharing his heartache over his parent's divorce, remarriage and final divorce. When he wasn't at school, he lived with his mother, Betty, and his stepfather, Jerah.

His father and stepmother lived in the same part of Florida, but he felt more comfortable living with his mother. His older brother, Troy, was in the military and stationed in Antarctica.

I opened up a little more and talked to Todd about my parents and my family life. Todd referred to my parents' disciplinary actions as abuse. I had never thought of them as anything but justified punishments for doing wrong. I had seen and heard a lot about parents who physically abused their children, but I never thought it correlated with my experiences.

My parents always explained their actions through Bible verses. They always assured us that God wanted them to do it. Todd disagreed and I trusted his judgment.

He was, after all, studying to be a preacher. He seemed to know a lot about the Bible and the correct interpretation.

"Do you know that I've told you things that I've never told anyone else?" I asked him one night.

"I know. I can tell. I appreciate your trust in me. I promise I'll always be worthy of your trust."

His blue eyes looked right into me as he spoke.

"I don't think I've ever trusted anyone," I said.

"It seems to me like you've had very few people in your life worthy of trust."

Suddenly, he embraced me.

It felt so comfortable to feel his arms around me and his breath on my neck. I knew then why I could trust him.

"I'll walk with you back to your dorm," I offered, as he released me from the embrace.

We walked in silence most of the way. There was just one last question to ask.

"Have you ever felt like you're different than everyone else?" I blurted out.

"Yes."

"How do you know what I'm talking about?"

Todd looked at me and smiled.

"Because I know. Didn't you already know that?"

"I've been confused about so many things lately. My attraction to men has always frustrated me. I get so many different messages."

My heart was racing. This time it was nervousness. I could tell that Todd was nervous, too.

"I don't know if it's good or bad that we've talked about this," he said slowly.

"How could it be either? We're just talking."

" I just don't want to make any mistakes."

My heart stopped racing. I felt Todd withdraw from me. Suddenly, I felt vulnerable and uncomfortable.

I wanted to ask Todd if he was attracted to me. I had to know if the feelings were mutual. His retreat prevented me from revealing anything else. We were already at the door to Todd's dorm, anyway. Before going in, he turned and looked at me.

"We've just got to make sure that we keep our eyes on Christ and don't give in to our sin nature."

I fumed as I walked back to my dorm. I was angry at Todd for making me vulnerable and then reminding me of our responsibility as Christians. I decided not to put myself in that position again. The exposure was too dangerous and too painful.

It was foolish to think that our relationship could extend into something more than a friendship. Homo-sexuality at any level displeased God. It was difficult to remember that my desires were wrong.

My talk with Todd left me feeling guilty. A feeling that was always there whenever I attempted to reconcile Christianity with my homosexuality. I also had anticipated that once I was able to talk to someone about my attraction to other guys, that we would have a camaraderie of sorts. It would help if I had someone to help me disseminate my feelings. Todd was hesitant to go any further than his admonition.

The pay phone in the hallway rang as I came up the stairs of my dormitory. No one ever wanted to answer the hallway phones.

"Hello?" I answered.

"Marc Adams in room 213, please."

"Hi, Mom, this is Marc."

"Oh, I didn't expect you to answer the phone."

I tossed my books on the floor and sat next to them. I expected a call from her.

"I just got in."

"Honey, we're calling about Debbie. The dean's office called us today and told us about what she's done. We're leaving now and we'll be there in the morning."

I closed my eyes and sighed.

"Why are you coming here?"

"Well, we've got to come and get Debbie. We can't let her do this! She needs help."

"Did it ever occur to you that maybe Debbie wants to do this? She's old enough to make her own decisions."

"But Marc, she can't just live with someone. If she wants to marry someone it shouldn't be a black man, either."

"I think she's going to do whatever she wants. It's her life. If you come down here and try to change her mind, she's only going to resent you. I think you'd be wasting your time."

"This is so hard for us, Marc. We tried to bring you children up right and then this happens."

Welcome to the real word, Mother.

"I'll tell you what," I bargained, "I'll make sure Debbie calls you tonight. You can say what you need to say without driving seven and a half hours to say it."

"Well, all right. But just make sure she calls."

"I promise. In fact, I'll call her now and make sure she calls before nine tonight."

After that weekend, there was only one more day of classes before finals. I dreaded going home for the four weeks of Christmas break. Almost everyone left campus for the holidays. The prospect of four entire weeks alone eating instant noodles and hard-boiled eggs held little appeal.

I went to lunch alone that Saturday. I was minding my own business reading *The Liberty Champion* when Todd arrived.

"Mind if I sit here?" he asked, already sitting.

"Of course not."

"You've been kind of scarce the past day or so."

"I've been busy, exhausted and nervous," I admitted. "But I have missed you."

I couldn't believe I said it.

"Feeling lonely?"

"Yes, I am. I'm not looking forward to going back to be with my family at Christmas."

"Why don't you come up to my dorm and study with me. I've got three of my finals on Tuesday so I'm buried. At least you won't have to spend the day by yourself."

"I'll be over around two. Is that all right?"

"No problem. I'll be there. Maybe you can quiz me on my Greek."

I went back to my dorm, gathered my books and high-tailed it across campus to Todd's dorm. I hoped maybe he would ask me to go with him to Florida for the Christmas break. I hoped for a lot of things.

"So you think we can afford not doing any work on the yearbook until January?" I asked, as we tossed Todd's soccer ball back and forth across the room.

"Absolutely. Who cares if we have to pull a few all-niters in March."

"What do you mean all-niter?"

"We just stay up until it's finished."

Without warning, a burning sensation flared up inside my chest. Something was happening to Todd, too. I could tell by the way he stared at me.

Instead of tossing the ball back to Todd, I picked up my pen and threw it at him.

"Catch that!"

I smirked when he raised one hand and caught it perfectly. The burning sensation ran down from my chest to my groin. I began to sweat. He threw the pen back at me. I attempted to repeat his catch but the pen hit my fingertips and flew across the bottom bunk next to me.

"Now, you've got to get it." Todd ordered. "Hurry up before we lose our momentum."

"Where did it go?" I asked, as I threw myself across the bed, landing on my stomach.

I could feel Todd's stare as I rolled around on the bed, pretending to search for the pen.

"I don't think I can find it," I said coyly, laying prostrate on my back across the middle of the bed. "You threw it, now you'll have to find it."

I barely finished my sentence when Todd threw himself onto the bed. He rolled on top of me.

"Maybe it's over here," he said.

The burning sensation in my abdomen turned into an explosion. I grabbed his belt loops and stared into his beautiful blue eyes.

"What are you trying to do?" I asked.

He lowered his face closer to mine.

"I'm looking for the pen," he whispered.

I closed my eyes, expecting him to kiss me. Instead, I felt myself being pulled off the bed. He landed on the floor and I landed on top of him.

I slid my arm underneath his neck and pulled his head up towards me. I was too shy to kiss him, but I pressed my check against his. The feeling of his warm skin against mine made me dizzy. Instinctively, I slid off him and began unbuckling his belt. Our hands were everywhere, eagerly consuming our first touch of another adult male.

Todd flipped me onto my back and straddled my chest. I stretched my legs out and my feet kicked against the door to his room. For a moment, I thought about the possibility of being caught, but the thought disappeared when he ran his thumb across my lips. There he was, with those eyes and that smile. I closed my eyes and let my heart take over.

Almost immediately after he climaxed, Todd stood up and walked over to the sink. He threw me a small towel and leaned against the sink. I wondered what was happening. I hadn't finished and he was acting as if it was over. I was shaking from the experience, but a different vibe was coming from Todd.

I sat up and leaned against the wall.

"Are you okay?" I asked.

Todd walked across the room to a chair and sat. Tears streamed down his face. I had never seen him cry.

"What's wrong?"

"Get out!" he screamed. "Just get out!"

I stood up, tucked my shirt into my pants and buckled my belt.

"What have I done?" he cried. "I've done something I never should have done. How can I go into the ministry after I've done this?"

My head started to spin. I was somewhere between total sexual frustration and disbelief at Todd's insensitivity.

"I don't want to go when you're so upset. What can I do to help you?"

"You can help me by leaving. You came over here today with the intent on making this happen, didn't you?"

"No way. This happened all on its own. Besides, you invited me here."

"I need to be alone."

I watched helplessly as Todd rummaged around the room for his Bible.

"Where are you going?" I asked, as he headed for the door.

"To the prayer room. Please don't follow me."

I did follow him out into the hall. I watched him walk down the hall to the prayer room. My knees were rubbery and my entire body continued to tremble as I turned around and walked out of the dorm.

There had been a point that afternoon when I abandoned my reservations and let my desires take over. I just couldn't believe that Todd wanted me to take complete responsibility. I felt dirty and ashamed. I had let God down by my actions. By letting down my guard and giving in to my own lust, I had done something evil.

I was thankful for the darkness outside. I didn't want anyone to see my agony. The cold wind stung my face and froze my tears to my cheeks.

Suddenly, something that sounded like a train

rushed through my head. I covered my ears only to realize that it was something inside me. I remembered that first sermon I had heard about AIDS, a year and a half earlier.

All I could think was that I had crossed the line. Surely God's judgment would follow. That pastor had made it clear that AIDS was the penalty for the actions I had just taken.

It was difficult to breathe. It was thirty degrees outside, but I pulled my coat off and fled to the nearest classroom building and into the restroom. When I had locked the stall door behind me, I stripped and surveyed my body.

I was searching for the purple spots—the cancer— that was a part of having AIDS. I didn't know how long it took to get, but I needed to see if it was there. There was nothing, but I knew it would come. I mentally chastised myself for not paying better attention during that sermon. I was sure that the pastor must have said something about how long it would take for me to show signs. Desperation took over my body, as I sank to the floor.

"Oh God, I'm so sorry! I've really screwed up this time! I don't want to get sick. I'm sorry."

I hung my head and my nose bled.

"I don't want to die for this! I just wanted to be close to Todd. I didn't want to die for it! Oh God!"

Nothing could have stopped the flow of anguish that evening. I had ruined my chances of making something of myself. My father had been right. I had failed.

When the emotional upheaval ended, and my nose stopped bleeding, I sat nude on the floor, wondering if it was just a dream. As usual, my keen sense of reality kept me from denial. My heart pounded in my ears. My throat ached from restraining my screams.

It was then that I thought about Todd. He would get sick as well. Because of my irresponsibility, I had lost my best friend. I had crossed the line. It was my fault. I should have been stronger. Now we would both pay for my weakness.

"But I love him," I said aloud. I knew I loved him. I had never felt so strongly about someone. Even through my anguish, I knew I loved him. I knew he didn't love me, but it didn't matter. I had to tell him. At that moment, it was the most important thing I could do. I had nothing left to lose.

I dressed and rushed out of the building. Snow was falling and the gusting wind slowed me. I stopped under a street light to catch my breath. I noticed Todd's roommate, Ron, driving his car down the road toward me. Todd was sitting in the passenger seat. I stopped walking as they drove by. Ron turned and looked at me and continued driving. Todd's head was bowed.

My heart sank. Todd had turned to Ron for help. I knew they were going off to talk or just be away from me. I hated Ron for being Todd's friend. I hated Todd for talking to Ron and not to me.

How could Ron understand what had transpired that afternoon? There was no one I could turn to for comfort or help. I didn't dare talk to Debbie. She could never know my secret. Loneliness reared its ugly head once again. I hadn't felt lonely since I met Todd. He had made a difference in my life.

It took all the strength I had to walk to my dorm

and crawl into bed. I couldn't do anything else.   For an hour, I wept alone in the darkness, asking again for God's forgiveness and for him to spare my life. My eyes ached.

I thought about the times I had planned to commit suicide. I wouldn't have to be angry at myself anymore for not having the courage to follow through.

8

Telling Brad I was sick sounded like a good way of getting out of going to church the next morning. Guilt and obligation forced me out of bed anyway. Todd, Ron and I always had breakfast Sunday morning and then boarded the busses for Thomas Road to attend the Sunday School and church services together.

Neither of them showed up for breakfast that morning. Ron was a by-the-book guy, and I wondered if he would turn me in.

They boarded the bus after me and headed straight to the back. Todd completely ignored me, but Ron dedicated a nod and a small smile. It may have been a nervous twitch. The burning sensation in my throat returned as I struggled to contain myself. I couldn't comprehend how Todd could be so cold to me when just twelve hours earlier, he was tearing my clothes off and getting places I never thought I'd ever let anyone go.

I sat by myself that day. I felt lonelier than I had ever felt. Dr. Falwell's sermon focused on an excerpt from his book titled, *"When It Hurts To Much To Cry."*

I listened carefully, wondering if I could gain anything. At the end of the sermon, I decided that since my wounds were the result of sin, I couldn't turn them over to God. How could I ask God to help heal the pain of Todd's rejection?

"I want to talk to you."

I turned to see Todd walking next to me.

"What do you want to talk about?"

"Let's just go to your dorm. I don't want to talk here."

We walked in silence the entire way. I knew my roommates would either already be in the room, or would arrive shortly, so we went to the prayer room. I locked the door behind us.

"I've been thinking all day about what happened yesterday."

"Did you tell Ron?" I interrupted.

"I haven't told anyone. I spent all day thinking and praying about how to remedy this situation. I've decided that we should terminate our friendship and only have contact with each other on a working level when we're working on the yearbook. Other than those times, I don't want to spend any time around you."

"Why not? This doesn't make any sense!"

"I've already made the decision, Marc."

He turned around and walked out.

I couldn't let him walk away without saying my piece. I raced out of the dorm and quickly caught up with him. I grabbed his arm, partly to stop him, but mostly to keep me from sliding on the icy sidewalk.

"I'm not going to let you just walk away from me.

I have things to say about yesterday, too!"

"Let go of my arm!"

"No, I won't let go! I can understand if you don't want to have sexual contact with me. But I'm not about to let you just walk out on our friendship!"

He turned and looked at me again.

"Watch me."

He stepped off the sidewalk and walked across the street. He disappeared into the Teacher's Education classroom building.

After maneuvering through a parade of traffic, I managed to get across the street and into the building. The only office open in that building on a Sunday evening was the education lab.

The door to the lab had only a small window at the top to maximize distractions. I peered in and saw Todd relaying a dramatic story to Ron, who was there because his fiancee, Mary, was an education major. I was crushed by Todd's lie.

I walked away from the lab and out of the building. There was no way I could, or wanted to, compete with Ron for Todd's friendship. I kicked a snow pile and jammed my foot on a chunk of ice buried inside. I was so angry, I couldn't even feel the pain.

Coming to Liberty had been such a big release from the personal hell I had endured in my parent's home. Life had become much more complicated. The fantasies I had conjured up in my head while a child were so much different from meeting Todd and sharing a real sexual experience. The ramifications for the real experience were much greater. However, I had not planned on having a broken heart.

The trek to my parent's house for Christmas was not an option for me anymore. It would be instant noodles and hard boiled eggs for me. I needed the solitude to get my life back in order.

I didn't see Todd again before he left for Christmas break. I had to sever my emotional ties to him. He was right about not spending time together unsupervised. We were too much of a temptation for each other.

I was able to work in the yearbook office during the four week break. I wrote a dozen angry letters to Todd and a dozen more letters of confession to God. I never mailed Todd's, but I certainly spent many hours on my knees trying to sort my broken feelings out before God.

My heart told me it was okay to feel devastated. My head and my Bible told me something else. I knew I had to follow the Bible. I hoped that my pleadings toward restitution with God would lease me some grace.

I awoke the day after New Year's totally exhausted and unable to get out of bed. At first, I thought it was the fatigue I had heard accompanied AIDS. I had to do something about my paranoia.

I couldn't bring myself to trust a doctor, so I walked off campus and hopped a bus to the Lynchburg library. Armed with three magazines containing articles about AIDS, I found a secluded corner and began to read.

Interspersed throughout the articles were photos of gay men kissing and one very moving photo of a dying man holding the hand of another man. The caption identified the other man as his lover. I had never heard of a homosexual partner being referred to as a lover.

I briefly questioned again my feelings for Todd.

Apparently, I wasn't the only man in the world who desired sex and companionship from another man. My conscience warned me that the lover in the photo had that deep look of sorrow in his eyes because he was without God.

The articles were sketchy when it came to details about the origins of AIDS, but they did state it was a sexually transmitted disease. That news was shocking. Not once had I ever heard a preacher say that. I pondered if Dr. Falwell and every other preacher I had heard speak on the subject was right about the secular media suppressing the truth.

My entire life, I believed in the Bible and what church leadership preached. I wanted to believe the doctors who had written the articles. At the same time, I didn't want to make a dangerous compromise just because I had a personal stake in the decision.

The article went on to describe symptoms of the disease. The descriptions of the suffering were almost too awful to read.

I looked again at the photo of the dying man and his lover. As much as I tried to fight it, I felt their overwhelming loss. They had wanted with each other exactly what I wanted with Todd. Soon, there would be nothing more for them to share.

Detached from my surroundings, I closed my eyes and prayed. I prayed that the dying man wouldn't suffer too much and that his lover would be able to continue with his life. I wasn't sure God would hear my prayer. I should have prayed for their salvation from Hell.

I decided that day that I had to believe the doctors over the preachers. The doctors had much more working knowledge of the disease and had day to day contact with those who had contracted it. As strict and Bible-believing as my parents and Dr. Falwell were, they never spoke of any other disease as being a curse from God.

All around me, people touted AIDS as a judgment from God because it appeared to affect a group of people who were, in God's eyes, living in sin. I felt calm after my conclusion. While I didn't conclude that homosexuality was right, it was almost as if I had been given a second opportunity to prove that I could follow through and change myself.

I decided that I would, once again, actively pursue a heterosexual relationship. I made promises to God that I would do everything I could to find a girlfriend and develop a serious relationship.

I also committed that, once again, I would quit masturbating. It was a sin regardless of whether my fantasies were about men or women. The closer I walked with God the more I would be like him.

I hadn't seen Debbie since the Saturday before she moved in with Wesley. I was surprised to see her outside my dorm on the second semester registration day.

Except for her bulging abdomen, she felt frail under my embrace. I noticed the dark circles around her eyes.

"How are you?" I asked.

"I'm fine," she replied. "I can only stay a few minutes. Wesley's waiting in the car. I just wanted to ask you if I could borrow some money."

"Isn't Wesley working?"

"No, he hasn't been able to find a job since he got fired from Saga. I've been sick a lot so I can't even think about working."

"You guys should have planned this a little better," I blurted.

"If you don't want to give me the money it's okay."

"I'll give you some money," I said. "I don't have much, but I can loan you ten dollars. This is the beginning of the semester and I have to buy books."

"I understand," she said, taking the money from my hand. "I'd better go. I'll call you later this week. Maybe you can come over for dinner or something."

"That would be nice," I lied. "Leave a message for me if I'm not in when you call."

I watched her walk back to the car. Her entire demeanor had changed. Her sense of humor and everything unique about her personality had vanished. It was like she was dead.

I reasoned that involving myself in her personal problems would be too much for me. I tried not to think about what I had seen and went on with my day.

It was a great relief several days later when everyone who worked in the yearbook office began drifting back to work. It was a good feeling to know I had made friends that were worth missing. While most of them were surface, business relationships, they were more important than anything I ever had at any other time in my life. It took being away from everyone for a few weeks for me to realize their impact on my life.

I hoped to avoid Todd as much as possible. Life

got difficult again when he strolled into the office two days before classes started.

"I want to talk to you."

"I would rather just forget about everything and move on," I replied.

"I have some important things to say."

"Okay, I'll listen. But let's go into the darkroom so we don't get interrupted."

"What do you want to talk about?" I asked impatiently, as we sat across from each other.

"I want to say that I'm sorry for blowing up and walking out of the prayer room like I did. I should not have ended our personal relationship because of something we both consented to do."

"What do you mean?"

"I mean, if there was wrong done back in my room in December, we're both to blame. It wasn't just your fault. I was there, just as interested in doing it as you were."

Just when I was ready to get my life back on track, he wanted back into it.

"I didn't really want to do it," I lied. "I was just suddenly confronted with feelings I had never experienced. My decision to explore them was my downfall."

"I know what you're saying," Todd agreed. "But I really want to be your friend. I think the friendship we've worked so hard to build is worth salvaging. I realized while I was away from you at Christmas break how much your friendship means to me."

I was beginning to feel confused again.

"I think we can still be friends, we just need to be accountable to each other when it comes to our attraction to each other. I don't want to go against what I believe is right. Besides, a few minutes of pleasure isn't worth getting kicked out of school."

"You're right about that. I was so upset when it happened. I thought I had ruined my potential for becoming a minister. Over Christmas break, I came to realize that God forgives. So, I had to forgive myself."

After our discussion, we made a commitment to be accountable to each other and spend time together praying every day. We also discussed the importance of pursuing heterosexual relationships.

The thought of Todd dating someone made my insides burn with jealousy. I had to do it, too. I just wished he would tell me if the idea of me dating someone made him feel jealous.

Within a week, Todd was dating Ron's girlfriend's sister, Anna. It was a convenient catch for Todd. He and Ron were good friends and their double dates allowed them to spend time together.

I began dating Lori, a friend from one of my television production classes. Our dates always ended up being more of a friendship experience than a romantic escapade. As much as I searched for it, I couldn't find within myself the key to unlock feelings of physical/sexual attraction.

I knew Lori was attracted to me and I could have pushed the envelope when it came to breaking Liberty's dating rules. I just couldn't bring myself to do something only because I felt obligated.

After about two weeks of dating, we talked and decided not to allow our friendship to disintegrate by trying to date. We managed to salvage our friendship.

I was holding up pretty well in the celibacy department. Lori was not a temptation and I had not succumbed to the prodding of my same sex fantasies. I was proud that I was able to walk close enough to God to keep that aspect of my life incident free.

My jealousy over Todd dating Anna faded. It seemed I was getting over him. That made me think that perhaps I was experiencing a change--at least a little.

I spent quite a bit of time with my RA, Brad, during the first few weeks of that semester. He had become a good friend but he was still an RA, which gave him the power to have me kicked out of school. I always had to remind myself of his position.

After I stopped dating Lori, I had Friday and Saturday evenings to myself. I spent most of them with Brad. During the weekend evenings, the dorm was empty and he was always studying in his room. He had an open door policy for everyone on the floor.

As much as I tried to fight it, I became very attracted to Brad. I had always had an appreciation for his rugged looks and his dedication to working out in nothing but skimpy shorts. The more I got to know him as a person, the more I fell for him. He was out of my reach, though. I couldn't tell if he was gay and I certainly wouldn't ask.

I often returned to my room angry and confused. I would have to hate him if he was trying to get me to open up just to fulfill his mission as a resident assistant. I had witnessed him do it with other guys in the dorm--even one of my roommates. He would get close to them and the minute they broke a rule, he would write them up. I understood that it was part of his job. I just couldn't let down my guard, regardless of how much I wanted to do it. The fact that I couldn't trust him kept us from becoming great friends.

"We should get together in here more often," I said, smiling at Todd.

It was mid February and Todd and I were back in the darkroom.

"We haven't talked very much lately. I've been wondering how things have been going for you," Todd began, ignoring my comment.

I shrugged my shoulders.

"It's going okay. I haven't tried to date anyone since I broke up with Lori. I've just been hanging out. How is it going for you?"

"Anna's nice. She's got some rough spots but she's not the worst girl I've ever dated."

"Remember when I told you I wanted to be accountable to you and not give in to my bad sexual feelings?"

Todd nodded.

"I remember."

"I've been very successful at controlling my fantasies and all. But no matter how much I try to ignore my feelings or lie to myself, I can't change the way I feel inside."

The confession liberated me from a monstrous repression.

"I wanted more than anything else to have sex with you that day back in December. There were a thousand times prior to that afternoon and a thousand times since then that I would have sacrificed everything just to be close to you again."

My voice broke and muffled the last few words. I bowed my head to keep from showing Todd the deep emotion racing to the surface. Suddenly, Todd kissed my forehead.

"I wanted it, too," he whispered.

I raised my head to look at him. He looked into my eyes and kissed me on the lips. Instinctively, I kissed him back.

I didn't expect to feel power behind his kiss. It was completely different from the female kisses I had experienced. Whatever it was, it was right. Soon, we were kneeling on the floor and I was pulling off his shirt.

When it was over, I wondered how Todd would react. This time, instead of getting up and walking away, Todd sat with me on the floor.

"That was a big experience," Todd said.

"Are you okay?"

"I'm fine."

"Are you upset?"

Todd shook his head.

"No. I figured this would happen. It's been difficult to keep my hands to myself for this long. Every time I've seen you I've thought about doing this."

"I didn't know you felt that way. I just thought you were changing."

"I didn't want to be responsible for distracting you. I thought you were changing. I envied you."

"This makes me think that we need to talk a little more and be honest about what we're really feeling."

"What we're feeling is wrong, though."

There was the guilt.

"I know it's wrong, Todd. It's just so difficult to control. Sometimes I think it's impossible."

"Nothing is impossible with God, you know that. We just gave in tonight."

Giving in had felt so natural. How could it be wrong?

"Todd, I've been doing everything that I'm supposed to be doing to stay close to God. I've felt like that part has been going fine. My spiritual life is the best that it's ever been."

"I know what you mean. This is probably the only area of my life where I cannot seem to find victory. You know, I see Anna all the time. I still haven't felt a sexual attraction to her or any other woman, for that matter."

Let's quit school and live together, I wanted to scream. Instead, I chose the prepared speech.

"Our Christian walk isn't supposed to be easy. We're cursed by our sinful, human nature. We'll struggle with it our entire lives. This is just another part of that struggle. Maybe we'll never fully have victory, but we're supposed to keep trying. Heaven isn't for perfect people. It's a place of reward for those of us who have accepted God's plan of salvation. You know this."

"Yes, I know. Do you ever wonder if it's better to just give in? We're going to Heaven because we've accepted God's plan of salvation. It's not because we've lived a perfect life. So, what difference does it make whether or not we've conquered this one thing in our lives?"

We were definitely at a turning point in our lives and our relationship. I had the power to manipulate Todd to do whatever I wanted him to do. Until that moment, I didn't realize I had any power over anyone.

"I think we need to recognize our humanness," I began. "It's easy to think that we need to be perfect. This sexual thing between us is wrong. It goes against the Bible and everything we've been taught is right. I think we should understand that while we may fail sometimes, we should still do everything we can to fight these feelings."

That wasn't how I really felt in my heart of hearts. I had to show Christian leadership in the situation. I didn't want to be responsible for destroying Todd's future as a minister by getting him kicked out of school because we weren't cautious. At the same time, I hoped what I said helped him understand himself a little more.

After that night, we didn't restrain ourselves anymore when we were together. Most of the time, we wound up together in the darkroom. After we had sex, we'd have a conversation about how we needed to work on not letting it happen again. There was no anger or guilt, just a polite chat.

We never mentioned our feelings toward each other. I think we were afraid that if we exchanged I love you's, that we'd begin something we couldn't finish. I said it each time I kissed him and I knew he was saying it to me when he kissed me back.

I knew that Todd wasn't having sexual contact with anyone else, so the thought of AIDS didn't come to mind very often.

One Saturday night, after working late on the year-book, I told Todd that I would walk back with him to his dorm. We decided to swing by the campus post office so that he could check his mailbox.

"Get anything?"

"No, but I do have something for you."

"What?"

"Shut up and follow me," he said, as he lead the way towards the railroad tracks that bordered the west side of the campus.

"Are you sure that we should walk through there?" I asked, knowing that the area was off limits to students for safety reasons.

"Yes, I'm sure."

Once we were walking on the tracks, darkness and trees concealing us from the campus, Todd took my hand and held it as we walked.

"No one can see us here. This is the first time we've been able to be ourselves like this outside the dark-room. This is what it would feel like if we could show how we felt all the time."

It felt nice. I pulled my hand out of his and wrapped it around his waist. He put his arm around my waist and we stopped walking. He got in front of me. I could just barely see his eyes in the moonlight.

At that moment, everything in my world was perfect. Todd brushed his cheek against mine and found my lips with his. He grabbed the back of my head to bring me closer to him.

"I'd like to stay right here like this forever."

"Let's do it," I replied.

He smiled.

"Okay."

Todd took off his jacket and spread it out on the leaf covered ground, next to the railroad tracks. He sat on the ground and reached for my hand.

"Come on."

"I actually meant let's stay here forever."

"I like my interpretation better. Come here."

I knelt on his coat next to him and pulled him closer to me. I kissed the top of his head. He looked up at me and I kissed his lips.

"Your heart is beating so fast," he whispered.

"I know," I whispered back.

We made love surrounded by gently swaying trees and illuminated only by the blue light of the moon.

9

During the first three months of that semester, I had spoken with Todd's mother, Betty, numerous times on the telephone. Todd told me she could help me with the struggles I was having as a result of my parent's abuse. She sent me the book, *"Irregular People,"* written by Joyce Landorf, a well-known Christian author.

The book was instrumental in enlightening me that I was not alone in my struggles to understand my parents. I still felt that there needed to be a better way to deal with family members who caused such great pain.

Todd finally asked me to go to Florida with him for spring break. I did want to meet his mother and his stepfather. Betty was always so nice to me on the telephone. The real attraction was the idea of being able to have sex with Todd outside of the confines of the darkroom.

I called my mother's sister, Lisa, who lived outside Orlando in Winter Park. I planned to spend two days with her and her husband, Tom. She was my favorite aunt because compared to my parents, she was sophisticated and worldly. Planning to visit her put my conscience at ease, as it meant that I could not spend the entire week in bed with Todd.

We hitched a ride with Ron and Mary for the thirteen hour drive. We left on Friday night, and before I knew it, I was standing in Todd's front yard with Betty headed towards me.

"Marc, it's so nice to finally meet you!" she exclaimed, as she embraced me.

That felt comfortable. I almost felt love coming from her. I wondered if she would have been so loving if she knew I was having a sexual relationship with her son. Todd's stepfather, Jerah, was quiet and moody.

We had driven all night, so Todd and I went right to bed. He slept in his mother's bedroom and I slept in his room. It was 6 p.m. Saturday evening when I awoke. I headed straight for the shower. I could hear Todd and his mother chatting in the living room. It felt strange to be in Todd's house and see him getting along so well with his mother. I was glad for him, but it made me long for a similar family tie.

I couldn't help overhear their conversation. Todd's voice carried well.

"He has been hurt so much by his family," Todd confessed. "I'm just going to make sure that they don't get the opportunity to do it anymore."

I knew Todd was talking about me. It was just strange to hear someone talk about my life. Now, Betty knew what life was really like for the preacher's son.

Long after Betty and Jerah went to bed, Todd and I were awake watching reruns of *Make Me Laugh*.

During a commercial break, we went to the kitchen to microwave pizza that was left over from dinner.

"Isn't this great?" Todd smiled. "We're free of the chains that bind us at Liberty. We can sleep in all week. We can do whatever we want and there's no one around to monitor us."

"What would we do that would require monitoring?" I asked, mischievously.

"Follow me," Todd instructed, as he turned off the microwave and headed down the hall to his room.

He motioned for me to be quiet, as we walked into the room. He locked the door behind us.

Within seconds, we were out of our clothes and in the bed together. This was our first opportunity to have sex without having at least some of our clothes on. The soft bed was much better than the darkroom floor.

I kept my eyes closed as Todd gently brushed my chest and face with his hand. At peace and unconstrained, I could have stayed in that bed and made love to him for the rest of the night.

We went to Cypress Gardens the next day. Our relationship had matured as a result of the sexual experience the previous night. A voice inside reminded me that what we were doing was wrong, but I pushed it back inside. I didn't want to acknowledge it because I knew what the guilt would bring.

The highlight of our day was not the water-skiing, bikini-clad women at Cypress Gardens. We arrived back at Todd's house about three o'clock in the afternoon. Betty and Jerah were both out, so we used the time wisely.

The afternoon sun was shining brightly through the bedroom window as we kissed and pulled each other's clothes off. In that moment, looking into his eyes, with the warm breeze and the sun, I realized how much I loved him.

I felt completely at ease with Todd, even though I knew we were treading on thin ice. I rationalized that, despite our sin, our friendship remained unharmed. It was simple to confess the sin after the fact.

We watched television together for a while and then fell asleep on the u-shaped pit group sofa in the den. We slept on opposite sides of the couch and I could see Todd's face. Just being around him made my life so much calmer.

"I love you," I whispered.

I fell asleep while watching him sleep.

I woke up two hours later to the sound of Betty, Jerah and Todd's voices. They were in the kitchen having a heated discussion. I couldn't hear exactly what they were saying, but it sounded intense. When they saw that I was awake, Todd motioned for me to follow him back to his bedroom.

"What's going on?" I asked, still trying to wake up from my nap.

"I can't explain it right now, but I have to go somewhere with my mother. I'll be back soon."

Todd eyes resembled those of a deer caught in the headlights of an oncoming car. He was very cold and couldn't maintain eye contact.

"No problem. I'll just wait here until you get back."

I hoped I had been reassuring. He turned around and walked out of the room. I heard the car doors close and his mother's car pull out of the driveway. Jerah had gone to the den to work on his computer. I headed for the bathroom to take a shower.

After my shower, I went back to the living room and began flipping through the television channels. Jerah walked into the room and stood behind me.

"Marc, would you like to come in and see what I've got on my computer?"

It was the first time he had been friendly since I arrived, so I obliged. Whatever was going on with Todd couldn't be too troublesome, I thought. Otherwise, Jerah certainly wouldn't have been nice to me.

Three hours passed and Todd and his mother still hadn't returned. I retired to Todd's room after I grew bored watching Jerah fiddle with his computer. I turned out the light and tried to sleep. It was another hour before Todd walked into the room and turned on the light.

"Wake up, Marc," he ordered.

Once again, groggy and confused, I sat up on the bed and looked at him.

"The shit's hit the fan," he said firmly. "It's over."

"What's over?"

"You and I. This thing that's been going on between us. Get your things together because we're taking you to your aunt's house and you have to stay there for the rest of the time you're in Florida."

"What are you talking about?"

"Get your stuff packed. You have to leave tonight."

"I don't understand."

"There's nothing to understand. We knew we might get caught doing this and that's what happened. Now it's over."

Todd pulled my suitcase from under the bed and began putting my clothes in it.

"I can't show up at my aunt's house unannounced."

"Then call her."

Todd pointed to the telephone.

"We're going by the church on our way. Mom wants you to talk to Pastor Starlen."

He turned around and walked out of the room.

I didn't want to talk to a preacher. I didn't want to call my aunt. She was hesitant when I told her how late I was arriving, so I lied and said that Todd and his family had an emergency. She promised to leave the key under the mat outside the front door.

In seventeen years, I had never experienced this kind of fear, including any of the violent episodes with my parents. We didn't say anything as we walked to the car. Jerah threw my suitcases carelessly in the trunk. His face was flushed. Betty was crying but didn't say anything.

I sat quietly in the back seat with Todd, as Jerah drove through Winter Haven to Northside Baptist Church. Todd walked me inside and down a hall to the pastor's office.

"He'll be back in a minute. I'll be waiting in the hall."

I didn't know why I was there. When the pastor, George Starlen, walked in and sat down behind his desk, I decided to try to take control of the situation.

"Why am I here? I don't know you and I don't want to be here."

"Well, Marc, Betty and Todd came over earlier this evening. Betty told me that she came home today and found you and Todd asleep together on the couch."

"So what!" I exclaimed.

"Todd admitted that you and he have been having a sexual relationship for some time."

I wasn't going to lie.

"What does that have to do with me being here?"

"Well, I'm here to tell you that you need to forget about Todd and get rid of your homosexual feelings. If you continue to live this way you're going to end up a lonely old man."

I couldn't believe I was hearing this. How would he know?

"If that's all, I'd like to leave."

"You can leave whenever you like. My assistant pastor and I would like to take you to your aunt's house tonight."

"Jerah and Betty are taking me."

"That's fine."

I bolted out of the office and into the hallway. Todd just looked at me, that scared look still in his eyes. We walked to the car in silence.

No one said anything in the car for twenty minutes. Betty chain smoked with the windows closed, making me nauseous. Jerah finally exploded.

"Todd," he yelled, "I can't believe you would do this to your mother. You have hurt her more than you'll ever know."

Todd was silent. He just looked out the window and cried. I couldn't believe that Jerah had been so nice to me. He was completely different now. Even though Todd had been so cold to me, I wanted to protect him from this monster.

"I'm sorry if I caused any problems. I certainly didn't come here to do that," I muttered.

"Well, you have caused problems. I should have known that Todd would make the wrong kind of friends when he went to college," Jerah growled.

I didn't say anything else. My heart pounded so hard I thought it might explode. They were removing me from Todd's life. I remembered how my parents and teachers had done the same thing with my first best friend, Stephen.

When we arrived at Aunt Lisa's house it was completely dark. I hadn't expected them to stay up for me but it would have been nice to have someone make me feel welcome. Todd carried my luggage into the house. I found the guest bedroom right where Aunt Lisa said it would be.

"Are you going to call me tomorrow?" I asked.

"I don't know," he replied. "I don't know what's going to happen."

He set the suitcases down and walked to the door.

"Don't just leave me, Todd. You promised me that you wouldn't ever leave again like you did last Christmas."

Todd just stared at the floor.

"I have to go," he mumbled, as he walked out the door.

I collapsed to the floor and cried into a pillow for two hours. God seemed so far away at that moment, I couldn't even think about praying. My heartache was my judgment. George Starlen's prediction had come true within one hour. I was alone.

I woke up around 3 p.m. the next day, still aching inside from the previous night's ordeal. Aunt Lisa and Tom both worked that day, so I didn't have to see them until that evening. After I tried to refresh myself with a shower, I couldn't help but stare at the phone, longingly.

There were no messages indicated on their answering machine, so I knew Todd hadn't called. I wanted to call him but I resisted. His definitive rejection of me the night before was fresh in my memory.

If the telephone would have rang with him on the other end asking for forgiveness, I would have given it to him in a heartbeat.

After Aunt Lisa got home, we went out to dinner. She knew something was wrong and tried to get it out of me. I didn't think it was wise to open up to her.

"It just seems odd that you would have to come here in the middle of the night," she persisted.

"Todd's family has been through several divorces and things are bad sometimes. You've been divorced. You know how it can be."

"I guess you're right," she conceded. "I'm sorry if I seem nosy, I'm just concerned."

"I appreciate that. I am looking forward to spending time with you."

"Tomorrow, I thought we could go to an art show here in Winter Park and then on Wednesday, we can go to Disney World."

Todd and I had planned to go to Disney World on Wednesday.

Before going to bed, I decided to call Todd. I closed the door to the guest bedroom and dialed the number to his mother's house.

"Hello?"

"Hi, Betty. This is Marc."

Silence.

"I was wondering if I could talk to Todd."

"He's not feeling well. We had to take him to a psychologist today. He's sleeping right now."

"Could you ask him to call me when he gets up?"

"I'll ask him."

As I hung up the telephone, I wondered what could have happened to Todd. He was usually spontaneous and fun. It was unlike him to go to a shrink and stay in bed all day. I suspected that Betty might not even tell Todd that I had called.

The next day, as Aunt Lisa and I were walking around the art show, I couldn't help thinking about Todd and how much he would have enjoyed being there. I worried about his well-being not just because he had to see a psychologist, but because I didn't trust his mother not to be doing things for her best interest, instead of Todd's. I wanted to help him but there was nothing I could do. The feeling of helplessness was the worst part of the separation.

"I found out today that there is a summer internship at my radio station," Aunt Lisa announced at dinner that evening. "I thought you might be interested in it since your major is television and radio production."

"I am interested," I confirmed. "I need to build up some radio experience. I just don't think I could afford to do an internship and have to rent a place to live."

"Nonsense. You could stay with here with us and ride with me every day."

"I'll do it. Do I need to interview for it?"

"I'll talk to Randy, the station manager, and see what you need to do."

"Thanks a lot. It's nice to be supported in my choice to pursue something other than religion."

"Your mother told me that they don't approve of your major or your decision to go to Liberty. I hear it's a great school."

"It is. I'm completely comfortable with my decision to go there. Although it does get difficult without their support."

"Your parents just need to get out and experience more of life. They live in a box."

I couldn't believe there was someone else in my family who agreed with me.

"Take Debbie, for example," she continued, "If she wants to quit school and get married, then I think she should do it."

"My mother told you about that?"

"A little. You know how your mother is. She never wants anyone to know that there are problems in her family."

"Mom and Dad flipped out when they found out that Debbie was pregnant, quit school and had moved in with a black man."

Aunt Lisa's fork fell out of her hands and onto the floor.

"Her boyfriend is black?"

"Yeah, my mother didn't tell you that part?" I asked, laughing.

"I can't believe it!" she exclaimed. "Your parents raised her better than that. What can I do to help get her out of that situation?"

"Why do we need to get her out?"

"She can't marry a black man!"

I almost vomited. Aunt Lisa was as much of a bigot as the rest of my family.

"I think Debbie's an adult and she's capable of making her own decisions," I reminded her. "I don't think that she would have moved in with Wesley if she didn't want to do it."

"Wesley. Figures he'd have a black name."

Anger ripped through my body. I couldn't take it anymore.

"Remember I told you that I came to your house early because Todd and his family were having personal problems? I lied. I was thrown out of their house because they think that Todd and I are gay."

"Oh my God, I knew it!" she exclaimed

"What do you mean you knew it?"

"When you were about eleven, one of your school teachers called your mother and asked if you were gay."

"Why did she tell you this?"

"I'm not sure, I think she may have been looking for reassurance."

"No one has ever asked me that question."

"It's not an easy question."

"Are you going to call my mother and tell her what I've just told you?"

Aunt Lisa shook her head.

"No, I won't. But I think you should tell your parents. Maybe they could find help for you. I don't think it would be a good idea if you stayed here this summer, either. I would worry too much about you. You need to be home with your mother."

I changed the subject. The situation was getting worse, instead of better. Aunt Lisa was even bolder than my parents. I tried to avoid spending very much time with her the rest of that week. I didn't feel like opening up anymore.

Friday rolled around and I still hadn't heard from Todd. I decided to try to call him again. Aunt Lisa and Tom were both at work so I called from the living room. The telephone book was sitting out by the phone.

As I dialed Todd's number, I noticed that my aunt had scrawled Northside Baptist Church and a telephone number across the top of the book. She had called George Starlen! I wondered what was said during the conversation. Just as I was getting angry, Todd answered the telephone.

"Todd, you're home!"

"Yes, I'm home."

"Are you okay? I called earlier this week and your mom said you weren't feeling well."

"I'm fine. But I'm not going back to Liberty."

"Why not?"

"I need to stay here. Ron will pick you up on Sunday to take you back to Liberty."

I wanted to ask if he really wanted to stay or if he was being influenced by someone else. I couldn't bring myself to ask the question. I didn't want to make him lie.

"Can I please see you before Sunday?" I pleaded.

"I don't think so," Todd said, slowly. "I've got a lot of things I need to be doing."

"If I write to you, will you write back?"

"Sure."

I could tell he was lying. The conversation was over. There was a sense of finality as I hung up the telephone. This time there would be no reconciliation. Hundreds of miles and loyalty to his family would separate us.

I wept bitter tears that night. I loved Todd more than I thought I could ever love anyone. At the same time, I hated him. The two extremes tore me apart. I knew I had to release myself from the bond we had shared. It seemed an impossible task. Regardless of what my Bible told me, I knew I loved Todd. My admission made the pain of the separation greater.

I begged God to take my life that night. I didn't want to continue my life if I had to live it without Todd. My passion for him had consumed every part of me.

When I awoke the next morning, I realized that, once again, God hadn't taken me. I tried to think about the positive things in my life. My life at Liberty began without Todd and could continue without him.

The ride back to Liberty with Ron and Mary was uncomfortably quiet. Ron was angry. He must have felt that I was responsible for Todd's demise. I pretended to sleep most of the way so I didn't have to engage in conversation.

I was glad to be back at Liberty. I felt displaced after Betty and Jerah threw me out of their house. My dorm room and the surroundings at Liberty were familiar and comforting. Liberty had become more of a home to me in eight months than my parents house had been in sixteen years.

I went to the yearbook office on the evening that I got back. No one was there. I looked at our working area. Todd's drawings and caricatures of celebrities, Dr. Falwell and me were posted on the wall around our drafting table.

His sweater was still on his chair. I picked it up and buried my face in it. It still smelled of his cologne. The same cologne I had tasted on my lips so many times as I kissed him during our lovemaking.

A memory of us working together in that office flashed through my mind. Before our relationship became sexual, my life was simple. I remembered Todd's concern about us sharing with each other about our homosexual feelings. He had said he wasn't sure if it was a good thing or a bad thing.

Apparently, it had been a bad thing.

The pain I had experienced since he left me at my aunt's house was unlike any other. I never wanted to experience it again. I certainly wasn't attracted to women, but my heart couldn't be shredded by someone I couldn't love.

Everyone around me seemed to hate everything about homosexuality. If I shared my secret with anyone, I would lose more than I could ever gain back. So much had been lost already.

I started building a wall around my heart. I would be the only person who would know what was truly going on inside. The pain from the loss of my relationship with Todd was too great. I was tired of going to sleep crying and waking up crying. There was too much sadness caused by trust.

I spent about two hours in the yearbook office mourning my loss, feeling sorry for myself and riding out a storm of other emotions. No matter how much I tried to make myself believe that somehow Todd would return to me, I knew the truth. Deep inside, I had always known this time was coming. No amount of preparation could have lessened my sorrow.

Brad was the closest friend I had at that point. I had to figure out how to pull away from him. He was, after all, a senior. He would be out of my life in two months.

I tried my best to stay reserved whenever he would try to talk to me. He had a way about him that made me feel like he really cared. That kept me from ignoring him altogether. I needed someone to care about me.

I was in his room late one night in April, standing against the counter he had just inside the door. It was a Friday and he had finished checking rooms for the night.

"So whatever happened to your buddy, Tuttle?" he asked, standing much too close to my face.

"He had some financial problems and decided not to come back after spring break. He also has a lot of family problems and he decided to stay in Florida to try to sort them out."

I looked to see if he believed my tale. It seemed like he had taken the bait, but I thought it was an odd question to ask, anyway.

"You and Tuttle used to do a lot of things together, didn't you?"

"Yes, we did. I miss him a lot."

I hadn't meant for the last sentence to come out. It was a subconscious thought that forced its way out. He made it so easy to tell him exactly what I felt.

For a fleeting moment, I saw what I thought was understanding in his brown eyes. Admitting to someone that I missed Todd, brought all of my heartache back to the surface. If I could have, I would have rested my head on his shoulder and once again, wept for Todd.

"Have you been working out?"

He walked around behind me and grabbed my biceps and pulled me back a little. I froze. I didn't know if he was coming on to me or trying to trap me. He stepped up closer to me and I could feel his body behind mine. I could feel his breath on my neck, his muscular chest against my back and that always interesting bulge against my butt.

I was beginning to sweat and I knew I had to answer his question about working out. I wanted to turn around and rip his clothing off, but I managed to keep control.

"Actually, I haven't."

He released me and walked over to his bed.

"I always think about going down to the gym but then end up not doing it."

He suddenly started acting tired by yawning and closing his eyes. I took that as a cue to leave.

"I'll see you tomorrow, Brad. Have a good night."

"Later."

I walked out of his room, hoping he didn't notice I had succumbed to the heat I had felt from him.

Closing the door behind me, I wondered if he was feeling and thinking the same things I was. I wanted to head to the bathroom and relieve myself of the sexual tension that had built up to an almost painful level during the fifteen minutes I was in his room. I wondered if he was doing the same. I hoped he was, but I knew I would never know.

A month later, the yearbook came back from the publisher and the entire staff had a party in the administrative building with Dr. Falwell and the college president, Pierre Guillermin. We had met with both of them several times throughout the year, but this time they were congratulating us for a job well-done. It was the first time in the history of the school that the yearbook was distributed prior to graduation.

I wished Todd was there. He had contributed a great deal to the book and deserved some of the attention. I was looking at the photo of the yearbook staff when Dr. Falwell came over to me and patted my back.

"Marc, you've done a great job."

"Thanks," I said, as I shook his hand. "We all put a lot of hard work into this."

"Your interview in the book with Dr. Guillermin is perfect. I think we're going to use some excerpts in an upcoming promotional piece about our faculty and staff."

"That's great. I'm glad you like it. He was an easy interview and didn't dodge too many of my questions."

Dr. Falwell laughed.

"Well, keep up the good work. I want to see you on this staff again next year."

Perfect. I needed more scholarship money.

"I'll be here," I promised.

"By the way, where is Todd Tuttle?"

"He left right after spring break. He had some family problems he needed to work out. Why?"

"I just wanted to thank him, too. He gave me a portrait that he drew of me. It's the best one anyone's ever done. I've got it hanging in my office."

"If I talk to him, I'll relay that message."

"Thanks, Marc. And tell him that I hope he returns. We need more young men like him going into the ministry."

Dr. Falwell moved on and began talking with other staff members. I slipped out the door and wandered around the campus for an hour. I didn't want to have to tell anymore lies. I felt guilty for not being able to tell the truth about why Todd was no longer a Liberty student.

I had worked so hard to get where I was at Liberty and I couldn't enjoy the few moments of glory I earned. A year earlier, I would have laughed at anyone who would have told me that Jerry Falwell would be congratulating me personally for something I had done for him. Now, I had to lie to keep from telling him something that would turn him against me.

Two weeks later, Brad graduated and was gone from my life. I was one of the last students to move out of the dormitory for the summer break. We talked briefly the night before he left, and he promised that he would wake me up the following morning before he left. He never did.

By the time I awoke, he was gone. I wondered what kept him from doing it. I couldn't entertain the thought that something more than a friendship would have ever worked between us. I still didn't want to live in sin--regardless of how instinctive my urges seemed.

10

Liberty Baptist College became Liberty University on graduation day that year. At graduation ceremonies, it was announced that a special scholarship program would be in place for the Fall semester. Any freshman entering Liberty who was a graduate of a Christian high school, would be automatically entitled to two tuition-free years.

It was anticipated that as many as five thousand new students would be arriving in four months. New dormitories and classrooms were scheduled to be built.

This phenomenal growth meant the student recruiting office would be busy all summer long. The recruiting office was located right behind the yearbook office. Many times during my freshman year, the two offices had shared parties. I had gotten to know the office supervisor, Julie, quite well.

The same day that Brad left, I went to her office at her invitation and interviewed for an open recruiter position. It was a much sought after position and I knew the work environment would be relaxed. I accepted the position when she offered it to me at the end of the interview. It was one of the most important jobs on the campus.

A student recruiter's workday consisted of responding to reply cards sent in from prospective students. A basic knowledge of Liberty and how it functioned got anyone through most of the calls.

The reply cards came from every state in the country and many foreign countries. Occasionally, comparison selling was required. Many prospects were shopping schools and it was up to the recruiters to get a commitment, a completed application and a confirmation fee to secure their place at the university.

I had connected with one of Debbie's old boyfriends, Juan, who lived off campus earlier in the semester. He offered to rent me a room in his house for the summer and I gladly accepted. He worked for the university's physical plant department. It was a great living arrangement, as his schedule was opposite mine.

During my training for student recruiting, I received a telephone call from my advisor Dr. Saxton. She said she had an exciting job opportunity for me. I thought student recruiting was the best opportunity available, but I agreed to meet with her to check out her offer.

She invited me to become a staff member and work in a television production effort. The Liberty University School of LifeLong Learning was a new branch of the university. The purpose of the school was to provide a means for anyone desiring a college degree who was unable to attend classes. The students consisted mostly of adults over thirty whose family or employment obligations kept them from attending actual classes on campus. My contribution to the effort would be to work on the video production staff to produce educational videos. We would videotape professors teaching their courses on a sound stage.

I eagerly accepted the position when Dr. Saxton reminded me of how taking the job would give me work experience credits against required television courses. I was hired for a floating position covering first camera and floor directing, as well as audio and editing work. The work was very straightforward and I was well prepared with the experience I had gained during my first and second semester course work.

The taping schedule alternated daily and my schedule in the student recruiting office was just as flexible. I knew God had allowed it all to work out. After thinking about how well everything was going for me, I remembered how I had almost believed my father's prophecy of my demise.

At seventeen and on my own, the biggest hardship I had to endure was my transportation. Juan lived on top of Liberty Mountain and I had nothing but a ten-speed bike to get me to and from work. It seemed foolish to get a car that I would only be able to use four months out of the year.

It was easy getting to work but not so easy going home. As I pushed my bike up the steep, two mile mountain, I spent a lot of time reflecting on my life and how lucky I was to be on my own.

Those times alone gave me time to heal. I still grieved over Todd and often longed for him. It wasn't just a sexual longing. I craved his companionship. I knew

I was still in love with him, but I knew that love would pull me away from God.

I wrote several letters to him but never received a response. I wasn't sure that they ever reached him. I contemplated buying a plane ticket and flying to Florida over the July 4th holiday. I had so many things to say to him that could never be said on the telephone or in a letter.

Saying any of the things I felt would open the floodgates to something much bigger. It would be my final admittance of my love for him and the end of everything as I knew it. I would be repeating the decision that Debbie made.

I was not willing to make such a tremendous sacrifice. God had helped me through the darkest moments of my life. I owed him much more than I could give him, even if I managed to live exactly as he desired.

But I still cried over Todd many nights as I journeyed home from work.

Debbie gave birth to a baby girl in late June. Wesley was at the hospital during the delivery and I had one of my co-workers from LifeLong Learning take me to the hospital after we finished taping for the day.

Wesley left shortly after the birth, so I spent the night in the hospital with Debbie. Every time I walked by the nursery and looked at my niece, Monica, I realized that I had a great responsibility to make her life easy.

Working in the studios at LifeLong Learning gave me the opportunity to get hands on experience doing what

I really wanted to do. It was gratifying to view a finished production and know I had made a valuable contribution.

One afternoon in July, I was sitting in the audio booth preparing for the first production of my shift when I heard the door open and then felt two large hands on my shoulders.

"How's it going, Marc?"

"Just fine, Dr. Falwell. I'm gearing up for another three productions today. We're completing Dr. Morgan's history course."

"I've been looking at some of the tapes and wanted to say that you're doing a terrific job. This has been a project I've wanted to do for quite some time. It's good to see it being done so well. A little later I want to go over that introduction tape I made the other day. I want to see your edits. Keep up the good work."

"Thank you, sir."

I watched him go around to each of the other staff members and give similar recognition.

I thought how admirable it was that he would take the time to come in and thank us. No one on the staff level reported to him. That moment alone with him again reminded me how fortunate I was to be on his team.

Working both jobs greatly increased my cash flow. I was able to put enough money in reserve to cover expenses for the upcoming Fall and Spring semesters. For the first time in my life, I had money of my own. I managed it carefully, as I didn't need to have financial pressures keeping me from pursuing my goals.

Since I worked continuously, I rarely had free time to venture anywhere except to the grocery store or occasionally to the mall. I struggled each time I was outside the confines of the campus. I was constantly finding myself making silent connections with guys. All it took was eye contact with the right guy and my knees buckled. The desire was sometimes so strong that I thought I would explode.

I just couldn't give in. I couldn't let God down by giving in to Satan's prodding.

I did manage to make it through the summer without submitting. I resisted the desire to have physical contact but I gave in over and over to my own fantasies when I was alone. As much as I knew that it was a sin, I still couldn't find freedom from its bondage.

When the summer drew to a close, I realized how much I had missed many of my friends who went home during the summer. The initial productions for LifeLong Learning were completed and that chapter of my life closed. I decided to stay on with the student recruiting office.

I enjoyed the camaraderie of that office and I looked forward to meeting the regular employees who were returning for the first semester of the 1985-86 school year.

That was when I met Alison. We connected quickly because we shared the same sense of humor. Our mischievous friendship spread outside the recruiting office and we began to spend a lot of social time together. I wasn't surprised when she asked me to go to lunch with her off campus.

"Is this a date?" I asked, as we sat down inside the sandwich shop.

"I hope not. I'm much to old for you."

"You're much to strong for me."

"Just because I'm on the track team doesn't make me a man."

"I've seen you and Carol down in the weight room working out. You're monsters."

Carol was a close friend of Alison's who also worked in the recruiting office.

"Carol can throw the javelin much farther than I can," Alison continued. "Can I talk to you about something? I need to talk to someone about it and you're the only one I feel comfortable telling."

"Sure. I love to spend my Saturday's listening to other people's problems."

"Just shut up and listen," she shot back.

I made a motion like I was zipping my lips shut which made her burst out laughing.

"You're so weird! But that's why I like you. Anyway. What I have to say has to do with my brother, Danny. You remind me a lot of him."

"He must be gorgeous!"

Alison stuck her tongue out at me and then became serious.

"He's twenty-four. A couple years ago he told me and my mom that he was gay."

Bingo.

"What did you do when he told you that?"

"I wasn't really too surprised. He never dated any girls in high school and I had suspected it after I met some of his friends."

"How did your mother handle it?"

Alison shook her head.

"She cried for two days and wouldn't talk to him for about a month. She just had ideas about what his life would be like and she had to change them."

"How about you? Did you have plans for him that got put away?"

"No, I didn't. We were fairly close before he came out. After that, we became really close. We've spent hours talking together about his life. It's been so difficult for him to make his life work. Everything around him tells him he's wrong, yet inside he feels something completely different."

"Does he have a lover?" I asked.

"No. He's had a few boyfriends over the past few years, but nothing permanent. I just worry about him a lot. He's told me that he's considered committing suicide several times. I got a depressing letter from him this week. I don't want anything to happen to him."

My heart already ached for him. I wanted to tell Alison that I knew exactly what Danny was going through.

"Remember I told you about my friend, Todd, the one who drew that caricature of me?"

"Yes."

"One of the reasons he quit Liberty was because he was gay. He and I shared enough for me to understand what's happening with your brother."

I wished I had the courage to tell her the truth.

"If he ever does anything to hurt himself, I'll feel so bad. I just don't know what I should say to him."

"There's really nothing you can say that will make a difference. As hard as this road is to travel, we pretty much have to walk it alone. Does your brother know you love him?"

"Absolutely. I tell him and show him all the time. It doesn't seem to make his burden any lighter."

"I don't think anything can make that burden lighter. Todd definitely couldn't find anything that made it easier for him."

"I worry about him getting sick, too."

"You mean AIDS?"

Alison nodded and tears welled up in her eyes.

"I know he has sex with a lot of guys. He's very good-looking. He tells me he's careful, but I worry. Lately, he seems content to be around his gay friends more than he does with me."

"I'm sure he feels a bond with those friends. As far as your fears about AIDS, that ball is really in his court. Besides, there's no guarantees that any of us are going to live to be seventy."

My candid comments surprised me. I wasn't sure I believed what I was saying. I must have, because I didn't have to think about what to say.

Alison must have known that I was gay. I could sense she wanted to tell me more. I wished that she would take initiative and tell me that she, too, was gay.

I thought a lot about Danny after that lunch. I knew the road he was traveling. At least he had been able to tell his family and there was some acceptance. I was chained to the Bible and my choice for my eternity. I couldn't shake that responsibility.

The next semester, my RAs asked me to be a prayer leader in my dorm. There were eight guys in my group. I had already developed friendships with most of them during the first semester. I had the responsibility of guiding their spiritual lives.

Many days I didn't have enough responsibility to guide my own spiritual life. But I took on the responsibility with enthusiasm. This was my opportunity to make a difference in the lives of many guys who I knew faced the same struggles as I did.

I specifically requested to have Peter and Kent in my group. Kent was a very young seventeen, and Peter was in his early twenties. Kent was very shy and always looked so confused. I knew Peter had already gotten him to open up to him. I could see that the same thing that happened to Todd and me, was happening to them. They just weren't fortunate enough to have the privacy of the darkroom.

Three weeks into the semester, their other two roommates got suspicious and turned them in. The administration got Kent to confess that he and Peter had been having a sexual relationship since they first became roommates the previous semester. They were kicked out of the university that same day. I helped Kent carry his suitcases and boxes out to the curb. I stood with him as he waited for the van from the dean's office to take him to the airport.

"I would go with you to the airport," I stammered, "But I have a class soon."

"That's okay," Kent said quietly. "You'd be more useful when I get off the plane and my parents meet me at the airport."

"Why?"

He started to cry. He rubbed his eyes with his fists.

"They made me call my parents and tell them what I had done and that I was being kicked out. My father was so angry, Marc. I know he's going to beat the shit out of me."

I wanted to hug him, but I wanted to keep my distance under the circumstances.

"I'll pray for you, Kent. God can repair the holes in our lives. He's done it for me many times," I offered, hoping he would understand what I was saying.

"My father's going to kill me," he said again. "Can you believe that they didn't even let me see Peter? They kept me in their office until he left. Now he's off to Michigan and I am going back to Iowa."

I felt his pain.

"Can you do me a favor, Marc?"

"Sure, what do you need?"

He wiped the tears off his face and chin and looked into my eyes. Then he looked away.

"Could you get Peter's address and mail it to me? We only knew each other here, so we never exchanged that information."

I had access to just about any information I needed through the student recruiting office. I wasn't sure giving him Peter's address would help him. After all, I hadn't been able to go on with my life until after Todd was out of it.

"I will do my best but I can't promise anything. Remember that as much as you hurt right now, you won't hurt forever. God can help you with that. Whenever I've experienced a loss, I've found that he's able to comfort and heal me. That's one of the things he does best."

"My father's going to kill me," Kent said again, as the university van pulled up to the curb.

"I'm here if you ever need to talk," I offered, as he got into the van.

He didn't respond. Tears streamed down his face and he stared straight ahead as the van driver pulled the door shut.

I stood on the curb for a few minutes pondering what I had just seen. Even though Todd and I hadn't been caught at Liberty, the memory of Betty throwing me out of her house was fresh in my mind. I prayed that Kent would find the same strength that I had found.

11

I was waiting in a short line to get into my history class when I felt a hand on my shoulder.

"Hi, Marc."

I knew the voice. I knew the weight of the hand on my shoulder. I didn't want to turn around. I stepped out of line and walked over to a bench and then turned around.

It was as if I had just said good-bye to Todd. There he was. Blue eyes and all.

"Hi."

I sat on the bench. I thought about the times I had fantasized about meeting him again. I couldn't think of any of the things I had planned to say.

"I'm in shock," I said slowly. "I never expected to see you again."

"I know. I never expected to see you either. But here we are. Do you need to go to your class?"

I did.

"No."

He sat beside me on the bench. I couldn't look into his eyes. I stared at the floor and looked up at his hands.

"Can we go somewhere else to talk? I'm very uncomfortable here."

"Sure. Want to go to your room?"

"Sure."

We walked from the building to my dormitory in silence. I knew my roommates would be in the room, so we went to the prayer room. After locking the door behind us, I walked over to the window. I carefully kept my back turned to him. I could tell he was just as nervous and uncomfortable as I was.

"What are you doing here?" I finally asked.

"I came up to visit for the weekend. I wanted to see Ron and Anna. I haven't seen them for so long."

I noticed that my name was missing from his list.

"Did you expect to see me?"

"I didn't know if I would or not. I thought I might see you if I hung around that building long enough."

"Well, you've seen me."

"You look nice. I mean, it's nice to see you again."

"It's nice to see you. I've thought about you often over the past eighteen months."

"I've thought about you, too. Many of things have changed for me. I've finally found victory."

I knew he was lying. Didn't he know that I could tell?

I turned around and looked into his eyes. My knees buckled and my heart pounded.

"I've changed too," I lied. "I've really been focused on changing my life."

Todd sat on a chair and crossed his legs. I sat on the floor on the opposite side of the room.

"So are you working or what?"

"Yes, I am. I've preached at some churches, too. Getting focused on being in the ministry has helped me."

"Same here. I'm a prayer group leader here in the dorm. This is my first semester doing that and it's been great."

There was silence for almost a full minute, as we struggled for words. I couldn't make up my mind whether I should punch him or kiss him.

"How long are you here?" I asked.

"Two days. I'm going back on Sunday. Now that I've found you, I'd like to have dinner together."

"Sure. Tomorrow night?"

"Sounds good to me. Can I pick you up here at about five o'clock?"

I nodded. I decided that I definitely wanted to kiss him instead of punch him. Everything about him that I loved before was still there. I wished he would walk over and hold me.

He stood up, and I thought for a moment that he might have read my mind. Instead of walking over to me, he walked to the door.

"I'll be here tomorrow at five. I've got to go now and see Anna. Bye."

"Okay. I'll meet you outside the dorm here."

He left the room. I stood up quickly and parted the blinds to watch him walk away. Then, I sat back down on the floor and tried to sift through my emotions.

A minute earlier, I felt like crying, but it had passed. Todd still had a hold on my heart. I was ashamed that I lied to him about overcoming my homosexual feelings. His dishonesty about his victory made me realize that we still couldn't be honest with each other. But then, honesty was what got us into trouble in the first place.

Todd's reappearance complicated my life again.

The more I thought about it, the more I realized I had changed a little. The last two days Todd and I spent together in Florida were very sexual. Eighteen months later, we were able to keep our hands off each other. The feelings were still there. We were just able to control them. Maybe I didn't have to get rid of my homosexual feelings. Perhaps I only had to resist giving in to them.

The more I thought about it, the more confused I got. Whatever it was, it worked for us that day.

"I should warn you that I'm broke," I said to Todd, as we drove off campus the following night.

"This is on me, so don't worry about it."

"It's been a long time since anyone has bought me dinner."

I had hoped my comment would spark some conversation about our separation. We didn't speak again until we were seated at our table.

"How's Anna?"

"She's good. She said to tell you hello. She said that she sees you a lot during the summer but not much during the school year."

"Yeah, that true. There's not very many of us here during the summer."

Silence. At least I could read the menu.

"I'm a little nervous," I confessed.

Todd looked across the table at me. There were those eyes again. He smiled slightly.

"Don't be."

"It's just that so much time has passed since the last time I saw you. We're both different."

"Yes. Many things have changed. I hope that we can put that all behind us. Maybe we can be friends again."

"I've never stopped being your friend," I said.

"My mother gave me every letter you wrote."

"She did? I always pictured her using them to light her cigarettes."

Todd laughed.

"No, no, no. I got them all. I couldn't answer them because I was going through so many things. The questions you asked didn't have answers. I'm stronger now as a man and in my walk with God. I can look at you now and not feel the same desires I used to feel. I've experienced a complete change."

I didn't sense that he was lying. Perhaps I had misread him the previous day. Maybe he had changed. That would make me the only liar. I managed to get through the rest of the dinner by making small talk and steering the conversation away from anything that involved us.

After I promised to meet him the next day before he left, I went right to my room. My roommates were out for the weekend, so I had the room to myself. I was glad to be alone.

If Todd wasn't lying about his change, then I must be doing something wrong. I was lacking something in my spiritual life.

"I have talked to you so many times about this," I prayed aloud. "If Todd can change, I should be able to change. I can't believe I lied to him to cover for my failure. I wish that when you said homosexuality was wrong, that you would have given instructions how to get rid of it. I just can't grasp what I'm supposed to do."

I brushed at the tears rolling down the sides of my face. It all felt so familiar. Tears and prayer always happened simultaneously.

"I still have very strong feelings for Todd, but after tonight, I don't think that he feels anything for me anymore. Maybe that's what bothers me so much. In the back of my mind, he's still loved me. I just thought we couldn't be together because you said homosexuality was wrong. Tonight, I don't feel that he loves me anymore."

That was it. That was why my soul ached. Todd had gotten over me. Until that weekend, I had found comfort in the fantasy that he still loved me. I needed him to love me.

"Please change me or take me," I whispered.

After lunch the next day, I waited for Todd outside my dorm. He was there, right on time.

"You don't look so well," he said, as we walked to his car.

"I don't feel too well. I didn't get too much sleep last night. I've got a lot on my mind."

"I still want to be your friend."

I nodded and tried to smile. "I know."

"I know you're paying for your own school bill and so I want to give you some money to help you out."

"Why?"

"I want to help you out. That's what friends are

for, right?"

"Yes, but I'm doing okay."

"Well, then spend it on something for yourself," he said, as he handed me an envelope. "This is from me to you. I should get going."

"Thank you. How did you know I needed it?"

"I just knew. I'm moving out of my mom's house next week. When I'm settled, I'll call you and give you my new phone number and address."

"That'll be great," I said, with as much enthusiasm as I could muster.

He stepped closer and hugged me. It was quick and friendly, but it brought back a rush of memories. I opened the envelope as I climbed the stairs up to my room. I hadn't seen so much money since I cashed my student loan check at the beginning of the semester.

I had to hope that this was Todd's way of expressing his love for me. Even if it was just in friendship.

My expectations were shattered after two months went by without hearing from him. I left several messages on his mother's answering machine for him to call me, but he never responded. He had told me that Betty always screened her calls. I couldn't even get through to her. I finally gave up halfway through the summer.

I pulled a letter out of my mailbox two days before that semester ended. The name, Kent Hurlon, was scribbled above the return address. I dreaded opening the letter because I knew I hadn't forwarded Peter's address to him. I knew I couldn't encourage someone so vulnerable to pursue a homosexual relationship.

"Dear Marc," I read aloud, "You were right, my

father didn't kill me. He threw me out of the house and
told me that he never wanted to see me again. I had to
bum change off people at the mall just to get the stamp to
send this to you.

"You never sent Peter's address and I understand.
I'd still belong to my family if all of this hadn't happened.
I've tried to see my mother and brother, but they won't
talk to me. I miss Peter the most.

"The good news is that I have found a way to heal
myself of this awful affliction (my being gay). When you
get this letter call the number I've left below and you'll
see what I mean. Thanks for trying to help me the day
that I got kicked out. You won't be forgotten."

My hands shook as I dialed the number. I could
tell from the area code that it was an Iowa number.

"Hello?" a woman's voice answered.

"Ah, hello. Is Kent there?"

"Who is this?"

"This is Marc Adams. I'm a friend of Kent's from
Liberty University."

"Let me let his brother tell you."

"Tell me what?"

I listened in horror as Kent's brother told me how
his brother broke into their house two days earlier. He
took one of his father's guns, stuck the barrel in his mouth
and blew off the back of his head. I dropped the receiver
and walked away.

As I mourned over the ensuing days, I thought
about the many times I had wanted to take my life. Kent
ended his suffering because he couldn't find a way out. I
wondered how I had held onto my life.

I met Patrick Canter, the second week of the Fall semester of 1986. He was one of the new freshman who moved into my dorm. I noticed right away that he had an interesting edge.

I requested to have him in my prayer group. It would be a good way to get to know him better. I requested a couple of other guys who I knew were gay. I didn't want to leave their souls to the mercy of a less understanding prayer leader. After what had happened with Kent, I determined I would sacrifice everything to make sure no one else did the same thing.

I knew Patrick wasn't gay. That's not why I wanted to develop a friendship. He was just someone I found interesting as a person.

He responded positively to my invitations to share lunch and other casual meetings. We shared common interests in music and other areas. I also sensed that he was fighting his own demons, but I didn't pressure him to talk. I knew he'd come to me when he was ready.

"Can I talk to you?" he asked one day, while we studied together in my room.

Finally, I thought.

"Go ahead."

He leaned forward in his chair and I could see he was struggling to open up.

"I need to talk to you about my family relationships. I'm having some real problems."

"Okay. I've been down that road myself."

"I can't seem to make them work right. I've tried my whole life to get my father to pay attention to me or at least make me feel like he respects me."

"You mean loves you?" I injected.

Patrick nodded.

"Yeah, I've never felt like he loves me. He might but he never shows it. We get along and everything but I feel like he's more of a friend than a father. I get along with my mother and my three sisters—although my older sister Lori has become a rebel of sorts."

"How so?"

Somehow I knew what he was going to tell me before the words even came out of his mouth.

"She was going to college to become a teacher and she met a guy and they moved in together. She had to quit school because she got pregnant. She's had a lot of difficulties with her pregnancy so the doctor made her quit."

I knew it.

"It's really caused problems in the family because her boyfriend is black and my family tends to be very traditional."

"You mean prejudiced."

"Yes," he said, nodding. "I don't have a problem with it, but some members of my family really hate it."

I couldn't help but smile as I thought about how to respond.

"Why are you smiling?" Patrick asked. "This isn't funny."

"I don't think it's funny at all," I promised. "It's just that since the beginning of the semester I've felt a connection to you. I couldn't figure out what it was, but now I know."

"Well, what is it?"

"I have a very similar situation with my father. I

have four sisters, which is very close to your three. I am also the only son, just like you."

"Well," Patrick interrupted, "to be honest my parents did have another son between me and Lori. But he died shortly after he was born."

"So did my parents. This is getting kind of weird."

"I'm scared," Patrick said, laughing.

"My older sister also was going to college to become a teacher when she met a black man, fell in love with him, got pregnant and had to quit school. Now, how do you like that?"

"It's almost unbelievable. The only difference is that you're older than I am and you seem to have adjusted."

"I've adjusted to some of it, but I know that most of it just takes time. The rest of it, including my nonexistent relationship with my father, may never get better."

"So I shouldn't always expect things to work out?"

"I didn't say that. You need to decide what things are the most important. Then work towards making those things work. It's unrealistic to expect everything to be perfect."

Patrick was quiet for a few moments.

"That's not exactly what I wanted to hear."

"I wouldn't say it if I didn't believe it. We should talk more about this. I'm sure there are some insights you could share that may help me with some of my situations."

"Hey, you're the hot shot prayer leader. I don't have any answers."

"I'm a prayer leader because I was asked to be one. It has nothing to do with having all the answers. I'd love it if you'd think of me as a friend. I can be more than just your prayer leader."

"I wouldn't have told you this if I didn't think you were my friend. It's not easy for me to trust people."

12

I noticed many closeted students took full advantage of the strict dating rules. The Liberty Way actually made it easy for gay students to lie about their homosexuality. I, too, was able to date girls and not feel pressure to have any physical contact.

At eighteen, my hormones were raging. Whenever I double dated, I usually found myself spending more time with the other guy than with my date. In several instances, the desire was mutual. But we didn't dare give in to the urges we felt so strongly.

After those dates, I always felt so foolish. I wasn't being true to my feelings. I was only being true to the God who created me with such an overwhelming blemish. I knew being true to him was the most important thing, which is why I continued to do it. It just didn't seem right that with all of the effort I put into maintaining my spiritual life, that my homosexual desires were still so strong.

I was doing all of the things that I should do. I

even wanted to change. Throughout my life, I had wavered between wanting to change and finding enjoyment in experiencing my feelings. But that year, I wanted to put it behind me.

I sent away for every piece of literature I could find that talked about changing from a homosexual to a heterosexual. The publications all proposed the same steps for change. I followed all of the steps and still didn't experience change. I felt like the Apostle Paul in the New Testament. He had a "thorn" in his flesh that he couldn't get rid of, regardless of how much he pleaded with God.

I spent one of the four weeks of Christmas break that year with Patrick at his parent's house in Ohio. While the drive from Virginia to Ohio was no fun at all, I knew Patrick was opening up his family life to me because he trusted me.

"So are they anything like I told you?" he asked, as we sat in his bedroom after everyone else was in bed.

"I feel like I'm at my parent's house."

"You're lucky though," he said. "You don't have to go home on breaks or during the summer. After next semester, I have to spend the summer here making two bucks an hour mowing lawns."

"Why don't you stay in Lynchburg with me this summer?"

"I don't have a job."

"There are always jobs on campus during the summer. I know the people in the human resources department. I could talk to them."

"That would help," Patrick agreed. "I would just have to convince my parents to let me do it. I don't think they would be very happy about it."

"You will just have to decide what's most important--their happiness or yours. I think that's a big part of becoming an adult."

"You're right. Parents just have this way of making you feel obligated to them."

"Why don't you pray about it?" I suggested. "If it's something he wants you to do, then you'll know. That always helps me."

A month before the end of the semester, Patrick agreed to stay in Lynchburg for the summer. I got him a job working for the physical plant at Liberty and we rented a small house about four miles from the campus. We moved in the day after finals.

Some mutual friends who were not staying in Lynchburg for the summer, let us borrow furniture from their apartment.

"It's nice your new boss let you borrow his truck," I said, as we carried our borrowed sofa into the house.

"He's pretty cool. Watch that corner there, Marc."

I barely heard him. A hot pain seared from the center of my chest to my back. I dropped my end of the sofa onto the floor as the pain moved up into my jaw.

"What's going on?" Patrick asked, setting down his end of the sofa.

I bent over and grabbed at my chest with one hand and my jaw with the other. I collapsed to the floor.

"I'm in really bad pain, Patrick."

"How bad?"

"It's bad," I gasped.

Thirty minutes later, I was in the emergency room of Virginia Baptist Hospital. The pain was so intense I couldn't lie still. Within a few minutes of arriving, a nurse walked into the little room with a huge syringe.

"What is that for?" I asked.

"We need to check the oxygen level in your blood. Now, hold still."

I laid flat on the bed. She took my left arm and jammed the needle into my wrist. Suddenly, the pain in my chest and jaw was pushed aside by the pain in my wrist. I looked over to see what she had done. The needle was sticking upright in my wrist right at the spot where my pulse beat.

My stomach began to churn as I watched her rotate the syringe slightly.

"That vein of yours is being ornery," she commented, as she moved the syringe.

Finally, the point of the needle hit the vein. The pain in my wrist subsided and the pain in my chest resumed full force. After drawing what appeared to be all of my blood, the nurse pulled out the needle, bandaged my wrist and walked out.

A few moments later, a doctor walked into the room.

"So how are you feeling now?"

"Exactly how I felt when I got in here!"

I was getting impatient.

"Tell me, Marc, how much cocaine have you had today?"

"What?"

"How much cocaine have you had today?"

"None!"

"Heroin?"

"None! What the hell is this? I'm in serious pain here. Why are you quizzing me on drugs?"

The doctor raised his eyebrows.

"You're showing some signs of someone who has just taken one of those drugs."

"Well, I assure you, doctor, that I have not taken any of those drugs."

"Uh-huh."

He turned and left. A few minutes later the nurse returned and handed me a small white cup. I looked in it and saw a thick, gray liquid. It was so thick that it hardly moved when I tilted the cup.

"What is this?"

"It's supposed to numb your esophagus," the nurse explained. "You may be experiencing a spasm."

I swallowed the nasty brew and experienced a dry heave. It took two tries to get it down my throat. The nurse took the cup and left again. Five minutes later, the doctor returned.

"How are you feeling now?"

"Well, the pain began to subside a little just before I took whatever that was that the nurse gave me."

"I am almost positive that you are not having a heart attack."

"That's a relief."

"Yes, it is. However, now we need to determine what exactly it is. I want to keep you here overnight for observation. I want you to come back later in the week for some additional tests."

"Whatever. I just don't want to ever feel like this again."

"You scared the shit out of me," Patrick said, as

he drove me home the next day.

"I scared the shit out of me!"

"So no news on what happened?"

"Nope. It wasn't a heart attack. But they want me to come in next week and take some tests. Hopefully, that will shed some light."

"Were you really scared?"

I nodded and sighed.

"Yes! I don't think I've ever thought very much about dying of a heart attack or something like that. It was odd. I kept asking God to take away the pain, but he didn't."

"Well, you're not in pain now."

"I know that. But I needed the pain to go away yesterday, when I was experiencing it."

"God always answers our prayers in his own time."

"That's what I've always believed. I guess I just haven't had an urgent need like I did yesterday. To tell you the truth, I felt like he wasn't listening to me or something."

"Marc, the hot shot prayer leader, is questioning God?"

I shook my head.

"I'm not questioning God as much as I'm questioning what I've been told about God. Patrick, there were hundreds of people in that hospital—all with their own problems and pain. Surely, many of them have asked God to help them. Where is he when they ask for help?"

"He's there," Patrick injected.

"Don't you think it's too coincidental that he's letting all of them suffer? Shouldn't some of them be feeling relief?"

"I don't know the answer to that. All I know is that I will never understand why God allows certain things to happen. That's what Christianity is all about. We have to have faith in God. We have to believe that he's not going to let anything happen that is too much for us."

The next week I was back in the hospital. I hadn't experienced pain again but I was there to take a battery of tests. After being poked and prodded for three hours, I was allowed to go back into the doctor's examining room.

"Well, Marc," the doctor said, as he walked into the room, "We should have all of the results back within a week. Hopefully, we can get to the bottom of this."

"Do you have any idea what it might be?"

"I don't. It's very possible that it's related to stress. How are things for you in your personal life? Are you having girlfriend problems?"

"I don't have a girlfriend."

"That sucks," Patrick said two weeks later, when I showed him the bills for my hospital stay and all of the tests.

He sat down at our kitchen table and drummed his fingers.

"Yes, it does," I said. "All of this money and they still don't know what it was. Seems like a waste."

"Well, at least you haven't had anymore pain."

"You're right. But now I have almost two thousand dollars in hospital bills. There's no way that I can pay these and go to school next semester. I'm just going to have to drop out for a semester."

Patrick shook his head.

"I think you need to make a certain phone call."

I thought about it. I had wanted to save that phone call for something very important. This was probably as important as it was going to get.

I pulled my wallet out of my pocket and pulled out a business card. I walked over to the phone in the living and began dialing.

"Hello, Macel? This is Marc Adams."

The study I was directed to at Thomas Road was much more modest than I had anticipated. I expected exquisite wood and fine carpeting. The only thing for me to sit on was a folding chair. I wondered what Dr. Falwell would do if I told him that I had fallen and bought gay pornography the prior night. The door opened and Dr. Falwell walked in.

"Hello, Marc," he said. "Macel tells me you're not feeling well."

I stood up, shook his hand and then sat again.

"Actually, it was a couple weeks ago. I had some severe chest pains and I had to spend a night in the hospital. They weren't able to find out what it was then, so I had to go back for more tests. The result is this stack of bills. I can't pay them. Liberty doesn't offer health benefits for its student employees."

"Okay," he interrupted. "First things first. Are you okay? What did the tests show?"

"Nothing. They said I'm very healthy and have an athlete's heart. I'm going to have to drop out of school so that I can pay these bills. I don't want to do that but there's no other way."

"That's why you called me."

"Yes. I was hoping that maybe you could have the business office defer my tuition or something. This is my last year. I'd pay it off eventually, but it would at least give me time to pay these bills."

"Let me see them," Dr. Falwell asked.

I handed the bills to him and watched as he carefully looked through them.

"I tell you what we'll do. I don't want you to quit school. You're so close to finishing. I will take up a special collection here at Thomas Road sometime during the next month. We'll take the money collected and pay these for you."

The marketing director informed the student recruiting staff that a gay magazine had published the toll free student recruiting telephone number as a prank. The magazine encouraged readers to call and harass whoever answered the call.

Most of the time the callers would scream obscenities at me and hang up. One night, one of the callers decided to talk.

"Student recruiting, this is Marc."

"Hi. My name is Barry Martin. I'm a priest in Cleveland. I'm sitting here in this city watching all of my friends die. Why won't Jerry Falwell spend some of his money to help those of us who are dying from AIDS?"

"I can't speak for Dr. Falwell. He does do a lot for people. He has a home for alcoholics, a home for unwed mothers and a ton of other projects."

"Before too long, there won't be anyone in the

world who doesn't know someone who has died from AIDS," the priest continued.

"I hear Jerry Falwell on television talking about how AIDS is God's punishment for homosexuals."

"He's referring to the fact that homosexuality is an abomination to God. It's a perversion of something beautiful that he created. He intended sex to be shared between a man and a woman. Every day when you wake up, you decide what you're going to do that day. If you make the wrong choice then you're guilty. It's very simple."

"How can you think that being gay is a choice? I never decided to be attracted to men."

My head was spinning. I couldn't believe the words that were spewing out of my mouth.

"God loves you even if you commit the sin of homosexuality. It's the sin in all of our lives that he hates. And he does punish us for sins we commit."

I waited for the priest to respond.

"A couple years ago, I met a man and fell in love with him. He was the only person in my life who accepted me as I was. He was the kindest, most gentle human being on this planet. He died last week."

There was a long silence. I couldn't say anything. It took everything I had not to tell him I was sorry for the arrogant, judgmental words I had spoken. As I waited for him to continue, I could hear that he was crying.

"I'm sitting here today, almost dead myself. I used to weigh 165 pounds. I only weigh 110 pounds today. I have cancer all over my body and I can barely see. You're telling me that this is God's punishment for me falling in love with the only person who ever made me smile?"

I swallowed hard to try to get rid of the burning in my throat. I knew that if I spoke I would burst into tears. What could I say? I knew the answer that I was supposed to give him would not make a difference in his fading life.

"Haven't you ever fallen in love?" the priest asked, quietly.

"Yes, I have. Once."

"Then you know that you don't have any control over it. It just happens without us doing anything. Didn't you fall in love with the girl without any effort on your part?"

It wasn't a girl. It was Todd. How I wanted to tell him that I knew exactly what he was talking about!

"I'm still in love," I said, wavering.

"And so am I. He's gone now, so I don't get loved back anymore."

"God loves you," I said, slowly. "I can promise you that no matter what pain you're feeling in your heart or your body that God is there. Would you like me to pray for you?"

A dull click was followed by the resumption of the dial tone. I couldn't return the receiver to the cradle for ten minutes. I kept my head bowed as tears spilled out onto my desk.

I had failed to be honest with the man about my own struggles and had failed to get through to him on the spiritual level I had been trained to reach.

Although I had the unanimous support of my co-workers, I still felt uneasy about the conversation. No one had ever called me a hypocrite but I was beginning to think it of myself. I couldn't believe I had moved a priest to tears with my judgmental words.

It seemed to take forever to get home that night. I closed the door behind me as I walked into my room. I turned on the light and, to my horror, saw half of the cover of one of my Torso magazines sticking out from beneath the sofa.

There was a naked man staring at me and anyone else who might have entered in my room. Suddenly, Patrick's cat, Winky, jumped off my bed and began pulling at my shoe laces.

Patrick had been home for at least four hours. He was in his bedroom sleeping but the magazine was sticking out far enough for him to have seen it from the hallway.

I panicked, knowing that this could destroy my friendship with Patrick, as well as cost me my life at Liberty. How could I explain the magazine in my room?

Two hours earlier, I had criticized the priest for having homosexual feelings and then there I was, trying to think up lies to tell my best friend to cover my own weakness.

I decided that if Patrick asked me, that I would tell him. If I told him I did have a problem and that I was going to the Liberty Counseling Center for help, he probably wouldn't say anything. I couldn't keep him from spreading the word to his group of friends but I didn't care. Any lie would be worth whatever dignity I was able to keep.

I walked over to the QuikStop convenience store a half of a block from our house. It was easier to go there than to the grocery store two miles away. As soon as I walked in, I noticed the manager behind the register. He smiled when he saw me.

I couldn't keep my eyes off of him as I moved around the small store picking up the few things I needed. I couldn't believe that one minute I was terrified that Patrick had discovered my magazines, and the next, I was making serious eye contact with the QuikStop manager.

He had thick dark hair that had a few obviously premature gray spots. His T-shirt and black corduroys were very worn and out of fashion, but something about his scruffiness made my blood boil.

His name was David. I could read it clearly on his name badge as I set my purchases on the counter.

Store mgr. —— "Hi."

I looked up to see him smiling at me with a terrific set of teeth.

"Hi," I flirted back.

"Is this all for you tonight?" he asked.

I knew what he was doing. And he knew that I knew. I would have jumped him right there except for the two rednecks outside pumping gas.

"I think that will be all for tonight. But I might need something more sometime."

He was going to say something but another customer walked into the store and asked for his assistance over at one of the refrigerators. He winked at me as he walked away.

"I'll see you soon," he whispered.

I smiled and nodded. I walked back to the house in shock. It would have been so easy for me to end my three year abstinence stint in ten seconds. Something was different about my attraction to this guy. It was more than just the usual quickening of my heartbeat.

The stirrings I felt when I saw David, mixed together with my discussion with the priest, made me think deeply about my life the following week. I spent an entire Saturday at the Timberlake house alone, thinking about the goals I had set for my life.

Three years earlier, I wanted to conquer my homosexuality. I remembered all too well, how many times I had knelt on a floor somewhere and asked God for freedom. Dating women, maintaining my walk with God and even watching straight pornography hadn't changed me.

I still found men attractive, and I had an increasing desire to pursue those attractions. It had been three years since I slept with Todd.

Patrick's compassion was a trait that Todd had shown. I was getting my relationships mixed up. I knew I was wanting more from Patrick than he could give me because he wasn't gay. He just wanted to be a friend and I was screwing it up.

As I sat on my couch that August afternoon, I knew I would have to make some changes. It was probably too late, but I needed to do it for my own sanity. I wanted to tell Patrick about my struggle with homosexuality but the threat of getting kicked out of Liberty was still very real. That bothered me, too. As much as I tried to ignore it, I knew the priest had been right. Dr. Falwell did nothing to help people with AIDS.

There I was, surrounded by a huge Christian organization that was supposed to be helping people and sharing God's love. Yet, they would never extend love if it cost them something. I was guilty of giving conditional love as much as everyone around me. My natural reactions were diametric to how I was expected to live.

How could I have argued with that priest when I was gay? I had thought my Aunt Lisa was a hypocrite. I was guilty of the same offense. While I was not a racist, I was guilty of turning my back on someone who was just like me.

I was betraying other gay people struggling to gain recognition and self worth in a world teeming with hate. I was also culpable of not recognizing the value and worthiness of everyone, regardless of their religious condition.

The change had to begin within myself. Somehow I needed to accept and love myself as I was. I had always believed that my homosexual feelings were evil.

The announcement that homosexuality was a sin came from people who didn't even know what it felt like to be attracted to someone of the same sex. I wondered what life would be like for me if I discarded the so-called "heart knowledge" I had gained from my parents, church, school, and Liberty University, and used my own brain to make decisions.

I decided to give David what he wanted. When I thought honestly about my feelings, it was what I wanted, as well. I wanted to experience what I was missing by not being true to myself. I also wanted to cut the ties I had selfishly put on the friendship I shared with Patrick. Perhaps I could salvage our relationship by finding in someone else, what I had tried to get from him.

13

I didn't have any idea if David even had a personality I liked. He had a nice butt and a sweet face. That was enough for me for the moment. By 10 p.m. that evening, I was riding in his truck.

"I just bought some property about ten miles from here. Would you like to see it?"

He's shy, I thought. How cute.

"Sure. What did you buy it for?"

"I'm going to build a house there."

"Oh really. Are you going to do it yourself?"

David laughed.

"Do I look like a construction worker?"

"You do have a Village People tape here." I picked it up and waved it in front of him. "You tell me."

He smiled while keeping his eyes on the road. He reached across the cab and put his hand on my leg.

"I've wanted to take you out to see this property since the first time you came into the store."

This guy was intense even when he wasn't looking at me. I put my hand over his hand on my leg.

"Do you really own property or are we just going to find a dark corner of Lynchburg to fool around?"

He stopped the truck and looked at me. Even in the dim light, his eyes sparkled.

"My property is two miles down this road. If you don't feel comfortable, I'll take you back. If you are comfortable, just sit back, shut up and enjoy it."

"All right, I will," I promised, as I leaned back against the headrest. After a few more minutes of driving, he stopped the truck again.

"We're here."

I couldn't care less about his property. I was relieved when he lifted his hand from my leg and began stroking my face. I thought he was going to kiss me, but he bypassed my lips and kissed my chest through my shirt. We were soon groping and undressing each other in the dark cab.

"The great thing about owning this property is that we can fuck each other in my truck and we won't get busted."

If I wouldn't have wanted to get laid so badly, his yarn might have made me nervous. We both got what we were looking for that night. It was odd to feel for the first time in three years, the same feelings of ecstasy I had felt with Todd.

When David dropped me off at my house two hours later, I realized that I didn't even know his last name. There were no promises made or implied that there would be a second round for us.

It was very different from my first sexual

experience. I had wanted to see Todd again.   I didn't
know if I wanted to see David again. He was nice, and
the sex was good, but I didn't feel the same tie to him. In
a way, I was glad I didn't feel any obligation. I still felt
free, still in control. I wasn't interested in falling in love
with anyone that day.

I tried to make good on my resolution to change
the relationship I had with Patrick, but it was too late. He
knew I was gay. I wasn't sure what led him to believe it,
but it didn't really matter. We never talked about it but I
could see the disdain in his eyes.

I probably couldn't be too much of a friend to him
after he figured out I was gay. Patrick was under peer
pressure from other friends to move on with his life. He
began replacing my name with "fag" and although he
smiled when he said it, I knew he wasn't joking.

The fall semester began two weeks after my tryst
with David. When Patrick moved back to campus, I
released him out of my life and we never spoke again. I
wished I could have been honest with him.

I began the semester without much interest. Most
of my friends from previous years had either graduated
or dropped out. The majority of upper class students who
I knew were gay had not returned. They were replaced
by fresh-faced teenagers right out of high school, who
had come to Liberty with the same expectations I had three
years earlier.

I sat in horror as several even had the testicular
fortitude to get up in a chapel service and tell how they
had been freed from homosexuality and were now pursuing a heterosexual life and an education at Liberty.

These were kids who were barely out of their

bed-wetting stage. I remembered how disillusioned I was at sixteen. I thought a new start in a new town in a sheltered environment would be just the thing I needed to set me straight.

I had been wrong and these kids were about to learn the same lessons. At night, instead of praying for salvation from their demons, I prayed for them to have common sense and some measure of luck in discovering themselves. I prayed even though I knew my prayers were rising to the ceiling of my room and crashing back to the floor.

My Bible, and the heart knowledge I had of Christianity reminded me that I was living in rebellion. Outside of a communal relationship with God, anything except a prayer of confession would fall on deaf ears.

It was interesting that a God who was supposed to be omniscient would take the time to discern between good prayers and bad prayers. It didn't make sense to me and seemed rather cruel.

I didn't want God to love me and listen to me just because I followed rules. Much of the Bible talked about God as being someone who offered unconditional love. The rest of the Bible promised that anyone who didn't play by the rules would burn forever in hell. It just didn't seem right.

I had at my disposal, a library bursting with books about everything that had to do with the Bible and Christianity. I spent every spare moment of the first few weeks of that semester in the library. I had a lot of spare moments once I began neglecting my classes. I spent much of the time researching.

It was the first time I spent any amount of time

investigating what I believed. Since the time I could hold my own head up, I had been force fed Christianity. Now, I needed to find out for myself what was really behind what I believed.

After a week of reading and taking notes, I was exhausted and discouraged. I had spent my entire life believing something I didn't know anything about.

No one had ever told me that the contents of the first few books of the Bible hadn't been written down until several hundred years after the incidents occurred. The stories had been passed down from generation to generation for decades until man had evolved enough to develop a written language. While I was surprised that I could locate information like that at Liberty, I was more shocked by the truth behind it.

There were books written by people mentioned in the Bible which had not been included simply because their manuscripts had not been located until after the King James Version of the Bible had been compiled. Suddenly, the concept of God speaking to me through my Bible had less impact because the information had been filtered.

My entire spiritual life was dependent on me believing a group of church leaders, who were as human as I was. During my closest times with God, I wouldn't have trusted myself to deliver a message from him to anyone. And observing the Christian leaders around me, I knew I couldn't trust them either. It could not have been any different with those who were responsible for forming my religion.

This enlightenment happened while I was studying in the Liberty library. The realization that my homosexual feelings were a natural expression of who I was instead of a manifestation of Satan hit me hard. I began to understand who I was.

The more I contemplated my spiritual belief system, the better I began to understand myself. My homosexuality was more than just an indication of who I was going to sleep with. My outlook on life was different than most of the people around me.

There were many students at Liberty who were gay. I just didn't know how many of them were active and how many were trying to change into heterosexuals.

I met Trevor anonymously at the River Ridge Mall in Lynchburg. I was at the magazine counter in a music store when I noticed the guy next to me was staring. He looked away when our eyes met. I recognized him immediately.

He was a member of a university singing group called the Sounds of Liberty. They were considered to be an elite group because they got full scholarships and were able to travel around the country with Dr. Falwell. They sang in churches and at other fundraising efforts. I had never met him, so he didn't know me.

"I'm sorry I'm staring, but you just look very familiar to me," he said.

"I don't think we've met. I go to Lynchburg College," I lied. "Maybe you know me from there."

"No, I don't think so."

He wasn't about to introduce himself. I could tell that if I was going to get anything out of this meeting that I would need to be aggressive.

"Why don't we go somewhere and see if we can't figure out why I seem familiar to you?"

I surprised both of us with my boldness.

"I know someplace we can go."

I put *Billboard* back on the shelf and followed him out of the store. I knew Trevor lived on campus so I wasn't surprised when he turned down the back hallway which led to the mall restrooms.

I wasn't sure that I wanted to have a sexual encounter in that restroom. But my curiosity got the best of me and I followed him inside.

When I walked in, he was standing against the wall doing some impressive handwork. I was happy to respond. He came quickly. Too quickly for my liking. I turned around and leaned back against the wall to experience my half of the deal when he grabbed my elbow.

"Sorry, man. I've never done this sort of thing before. I have to get out of here. Sorry."

Then he ran out the door.

Frustrated, I washed my hands and left the restroom. Apparently, he was one of the students at Liberty who was running from the truth about himself. I was able to understand his anxiety above my own frustration.

I felt sorry for him. He was older than me and he still hadn't come to terms with his sexuality. The girlfriend he kept was now an obvious cover.

A week later, another member of the Sounds of Liberty, Darin Bott, was expelled for being gay. Darin was a friend of Alison's. She told me that he had been caught taking a shower with his lover off campus at his lover's apartment.

Dean Baker and several other school officials kicked in the apartment door to catch them in the act.

Another gay student who had been caught, sold Darin out as part of a deal. The administration guaranteed him immunity for his crime if he would turn in everyone else he knew. Darin's lover agreed to get counseling from the Liberty Counseling Center, but Darin refused.

Alison said he told Dean Baker that he had always been gay and always would be. He was shipped back to Atlanta the same day.

I didn't think I would have had the courage to stand up to Dean Baker (once again) and proudly herald my gayness. I knew what would happen to the weak relationships I had with my family, not to mention my friends from Liberty. I had already screwed up my friendship with Patrick.

Two weeks into that semester, Debbie left Wesley and took Monica to Pennsylvania. She was eight months pregnant.

Debbie claimed that Wesley was cheating on her and couldn't keep a job. My parents allowed her to stay at their house for a couple weeks until she got her own place.

Thanks to her welfare status and a hefty check I sent for her security deposit, she was able to rent a house in Wilkes-Barre. Within a week after moving into the house, Wesley moved back in with her and the children.

Carol told me in a letter that Debbie had called him and invited him back, even though she knew for a fact that he had been having affairs.

Debbie gave birth to Wesley, Jr. in October. Wesley wasn't even at the hospital when his third child was born. Carol said that Debbie claimed he was at work, but she wasn't very convincing.

14

I loved to take walks at night when there was a strong, warm breeze. There was nothing so invigorating. During those quiet times alone, I felt what I thought was the comforting hand of God on my often hurting heart. I was indeed lonely.

The joy of the freedom I had experienced when I first started school had faded. Worse, I knew I was a hypocrite. All of the things that I was pretending to be just did not work. I had felt this before, but never so strongly. A small seed of discontent was growing deep inside.

I struggled constantly between my desire to live as a fundamentalist Christian and my instinctive feelings. I was tiring of hearing sermon after sermon filled with venomous hatred toward everyone around me.

I needed a sign, something that would give me direction. The turmoil inside me was beginning to take its toll. Depression came very easily and there wasn't much that would make me feel better.

I wanted the pieces of my life to fit together instead of being in a jumbled mess. As I tried to put them together, they just wouldn't fit. My religion made all of the pieces exactly alike. There were no edges to find, just piece after piece.

I decided to assemble the pieces as if I had no religious knowledge. First of all, I wouldn't belong at Liberty University. I would be able to live on my own, most likely somewhere in California. I would be able to end the turmoil over my sexuality.

Without the fundamentalist ideology, I could live as a gay man and feel content and proud instead of inferior and troubled. I would also be able to go through life without having Jerry Falwell's signature on a college degree that I would have to show everyone. I knew that would cost me something somewhere down the road.

The idea of having just a few of the pieces fit together, sent a chill through my body. It meant that I would lose everything I had that I ever thought meant anything to me. I knew how my family and friends would respond to my coming out. It would be an enormous step to leave the security of being in college to go into the real world.

The more I thought about it, the more I realized that it was what I had to do. It was the first step toward freedom. But I didn't want to do it so suddenly that I couldn't keep control of my world. I didn't want the loss that would accompany it to be more than I was able to handle.

Almost immediately, I began to think about the steps I needed to take to gain my freedom. My main goal after finishing college was to go straight to California. A mental review of my wallet and bank account let me know that it would be foolish to even try to do that at that point. As much as I wanted to ignore it, the reality of what I was going to have to do finally sunk in.

The idea of returning to live with my parents made me nauseous. I couldn't think of any other way to live inexpensively so that I could put enough money away to move to California. I knew they had converted the church into a studio apartment. It couldn't be too intolerable for a few months, I reasoned.

Under no circumstances, did I want to give my parents the impression that I was returning to the nest because I had failed at Liberty. I had to swallow a lot of pride to make the decision to move back in with my parents. It was the only way.

For the first time, I regretted attending Liberty. I knew I had learned much about myself while I was there but the cost had been great. I had sacrificed everything to go there. Three and a half years later, one semester from graduation, I was throwing in the towel because Jerry Falwell and everyone else at Liberty hated people like me. Without being as blatant, I was doing exactly what Darin Bott had done.

I returned to my parent's house for Thanksgiving break. I decided to break myself back in slowly. Telling my parents and my sisters that I was leaving Liberty and returning home for a few months was humiliating. On one hand, I was returning to Pennsylvania and the house I swore I'd never return to, but on the other, I was returning on my own terms. I was doing what was convenient for me. I just wished I could tell them I was gay.

"Why don't you want to finish?" Carol asked me,

when we were sitting alone in her room.

"I've had enough. I don't feel like I belong there anymore. There was a time when I would never have been able to leave. But I've outgrown it. I just want to focus on getting to California. When I get there, maybe I'll pick up where I left off."

"Just because I'm putting a hold on getting a piece of paper with the word degree written on it, doesn't mean that you should do the same. Being a nurse is a lot more complicated than making television programs or designing ads. Besides, you need to get out of this house the same way I did. College is your only freedom. You need to do it."

"Believe me," she laughed, "there's nothing you or anyone else could say that would keep me from going to college. I want to get out of here."

We both jumped when the telephone rang. Carol grabbed it.

"Hello? Hi, Debbie. What's wrong? Why don't you call the police?" Carol yelled.

"What's wrong?" I tried to interrupt.

Carol put her hand over the mouthpiece.

"Wesley came home drunk and when Debbie threatened to leave, he pulled out a knife and now he won't let her leave."

"Debbie, we'll call the police," Carol said.

I grabbed the telephone out of Carol's hand.

"Debbie, do you need us to come over there? We'll call the police."

"Don't call the police, please. Wesley just doesn't want me to leave with the kids."

"This is crazy, Debbie. I'm calling the police."

I heard a struggle on the other end.

"Hello? Hello? Is that you Marc?"

"Yes. Now you either let Debbie and the kids walk out of that house now or I'm going to call the police."

"Shut the fuck up," Wesley yelled. "Why don't you get your faggot ass over here and say that to my face!" he challenged.

Stunned by his choice of words for me, I threw the telephone on the floor and walked away. I wanted to run as far away as I could go, but there was nowhere to run. There was nowhere to go where I could find rest from my burden. I walked out of the house, not caring what happened to Debbie or her children. I had done enough.

Wesley eventually let Debbie and the kids leave. As she had done every other time, Debbie returned to him after a couple hours.

Three days later, I was back at Liberty wondering how I would survive the next stage of my life. I had two weeks of classes and then one week of finals before I was free. When I made the announcement to my friends that I was leaving, I lied and told them that it was because I didn't have the money to stay. I wished I could have told them the truth.

It was difficult to pack my things. I had spent so much time at Liberty and in Lynchburg that I had to fight back some feelings of insecurity. I knew I was heading into the real world. For the next six months, my real world would be Shavertown.

A week after Christmas I wrote a letter to a man who published several gay erotic magazines. I had no idea that magazines such as *The Advocate* even existed. I only had access to a very limited selection of gay   pornography at a couple adult stores around Wilkes-Barre.

The gist of my letter explained who I was and where I was coming from. I wrote about being a Liberty student and my rearing as a preacher's son. I wanted to test the waters and see if the publisher knew of any other magazines that would publish a series of articles I wanted to write.

I was surprised to receive a call from the publisher's assistant within a week. My mother answered the telephone and the assistant, Kelly, was very discreet and said he was responding to an article I had queried.

"Hello?"

"Hi, this is Kelly. I'm David Hartman's assistant. He received your letter regarding the article you wanted to write."

"Oh yes. Actually, I was interested in writing a series of articles."

"I'm interested in your life at Jerry Falwell's college. Did anyone there know you were gay?"

I was puzzled by his inquisitiveness. I didn't want to give away too much information before I wrote the articles.

"If I would have let anyone know I was gay, I would have been expelled."

"Was there an underground gay network there?"

I could tell this guy had spent way too much time reading sensational news and probably had never talked to a true fundamentalist Christian.

"There were no networks of people. It's Jerry Falwell's university. People go there because they want to live holy lives. Homosexuality is evil to them."

I think he sensed my impatience. I was impatient. This guy was digging for dirt on Jerry Falwell instead of having an interest in what I had to offer. The conversation ended rather abruptly and I never pursued writing the articles. I figured I'd find someone to publish the articles after I moved to LA.

15

I got a job as a waiter at Chi-Chi's Mexican Restaurant in Wilkes-Barre. I was shopping in Boscov's department store in downtown Wilkes-Barre, looking for black pants for my job when I saw Ryan.

He was working in the men's clothing department. I saw him without him noticing me. He was about forty years old and I thought it was odd that I was attracted to someone so much older than me.

His mannerisms reminded me of David. I wondered if the rest of him would remind me of David.

I waited until all of the other customers had left the department. Then I took the pants I had chosen over to his register.

"Rough night?" I hoped he would notice me.

He noticed.

"It's not even the kind of rough I enjoy. Is this all for you?" he asked, taking my pants from me.

His eyes never left mine.

"That's all. I may bring these back tomorrow to

have the tailor fit them a little better. I saw the sign that he's only here weekdays."

I looked at his nameplate to see his name.

"That's right. But I can mark all of the measurements now if you like. Then I'll leave it for the tailor to start working on tomorrow. It'll save you a trip."

"That would be great. I didn't realize you could do that," I said, as we walked over to the fitting rooms.

"I'm skilled at doing more than just checking people out."

"That's good to know," I smiled. "Let me try these on and I'll be right out."

I was more than ready to have him measure me. We were both enjoying the flirting. He was smiling a big smile and holding the measuring tape when I went back out.

"I don't think that tape is long enough," I joked.

"Oh, please! Like I haven't heard that one a million times."

"Sorry. Just trying to be friendly. My name's Marc Adams."

"Ryan Gannett," he answered, as he worked on the cuffs. "Do you work around here?"

"Actually, on Monday, I'm starting a new job at Chi-Chi's near the Wyoming Valley Mall."

"I saw that they were building one. I'm originally from St. Louis and that's where their headquarters are located. Good food."

The banter continued until he began measuring my inseam. "My God!" he exclaimed. "I am going to need a longer tape!"

"Okay, so it was a recycled joke, let's drop it."

"If I give you my telephone number will you forget it?" he asked quickly, looking up at me.

"Absolutely not," I promised. "In fact, when the store closes tonight, why don't you give me your number. I don't have anything to write it down with now but perhaps you have a place where I can do that."

"Yes, I do."

Ryan lived in Kingston, just over the Market Street bridge from downtown Wilkes-Barre. Ironically, it was in a building located next to the bank where I had received my student loans to attend Liberty. I knew the area well.

His apartment was small but very comfortable. I immediately noticed photographs of him with another man on the walls.

"That's my lover, Kevin," he said, quietly. He was killed in a car accident four months ago."

"I'm sorry," I said quickly.

"A drunk driver," he commented.

"One of my roommates in college had a brother who was killed by a drunk driver."

"Kevin was the drunk driver. He was coming down Larksville Mountain and completely missed a turn. I'll never forgive him," he said, wistfully.

"I'm sorry if I brought up a sensitive subject."

"You didn't do anything wrong."

He put his right arm across my shoulder and his left arm around the front of my waist. It felt good to be close to a man again. I returned the embrace and tried to take control of the situation. My efforts were thwarted as Ryan took over. All I had to do was sit back and enjoy. I closed my eyes and went straight to Heaven.

I climaxed quickly and was startled out of my fantasy by the sound of Ryan choking. At first, I thought he might be continuing the measuring tape joke, but he wasn't.

His flushed face twisted as he grabbed at his chest and slumped onto the floor. I kneeled on the floor next to him and turned his face.

His eyes were wide open and lifeless. He wasn't breathing and I couldn't feel a pulse. I found a telephone on a nearby table and frantically called 911.

"I need an ambulance here right away!" I shouted.

"What is the address?"

What was the address?

I remembered the bank and gave her that address.

"It's the apartment building next door. Apartment number six. You've got to hurry. I-I think he's dead."

"I'm sending the ambulance now, sir. What is your name?"

"David Miller," I lied.

"Is he breathing David?"

"No, he's not. I think he had a heart attack. I know he's dead. But please hurry and send the ambulance."

"I want to stay on the line with you until the ambulance gets there. Do you know CPR?"

I didn't.

The emergency operator walked me through the steps. Every time I pressed my lips against Ryan's mouth, I felt nothing but cold flesh. When I pumped my fist on his chest, there was no resistance.

As soon as I heard the ambulance arrive and the paramedics enter the building, I rushed into the hall.

"Hurry up!," I yelled. "He's in apartment six. I think he's had a heart attack."

After my yelling, several of Ryan's neighbors opened their doors and walked into the hall.

"What's going on?" one of them asked.

I walked out of the building for some air. I found a tree to hide behind and vomited.

Two hours later, I made my way back across the bridge to downtown Wilkes-Barre to catch a bus back to Shavertown. The usual thirty minute ride seemed to last hours.

All I could hope for was that somehow Ryan and his lover were together. It was the only way I could retain my sanity that night. A few days later, I stood in the shade of a large tree in the cemetery and observed his funeral. I wondered if everyone there was wondering what happened to Ryan.

Fear kept me from talking to any of them.

I threw myself into my new job to try and forget about what had happened to Ryan. I was only a waiter, but with the experience I had from my job at Liberty, I was also going to be a trainer.

Oddly enough, I was the only waiter, or employee for that matter, who was gay. Most of the people I was working with were easy to get along with, but I didn't think I would ever feel comfortable coming out to any of them. I wasn't working to make friends, I constantly reminded myself. I was working to save enough money to move to California.

Every employee went through a rigorous three week training period before the restaurant opened. When I had successfully completed the training I was ready to begin working. I just wasn't ready for what happened two weeks into the job.

I began with my usual greeting.

"Hello, welcome to Chi-Chi's. Can I start you off with something from the bar?"

I raised my head to see Mr. Wonderful sitting in front of me. I had to take a deep breath and lean up against the booth to keep from falling.

"I don't think so. I'll just have an iced tea and number forty-seven," he replied, pointing to the menu. "I'm kind of in a rush, so if you could get it to me as quickly as possible, I'd appreciate it."

"No problem," I managed to smile back at him.

He pushed his shoulder-length black hair back away from his eyes. This guy knew exactly what he was doing. I hoped what I was feeling inside wasn't showing on my face. I couldn't keep from staring into his eyes which were so blue and captivating they should have been illegal.

I turned around quickly and walked back toward the kitchen to place the order. I had to see if he was watching. I turned my head and looked back. He was watching and smiling. From that point on, it didn't matter if I was showing how I felt because he wasn't holding back his feelings. I couldn't let him get away. I was curious to discover the mystery behind those beautiful blues.

I hadn't felt so much desire for someone since Todd. I knew this guy was waiting for me to make the first move. At the same time, my head reminded me about the experience with Ryan.

"My name's Marc. I hope when you come back you'll ask for one of my tables."

"My name is Richard and I hope you'll call me when you're off work tonight."

He pushed a piece of paper with his telephone number written on it.

"I'm off at three. Just be there when I call," I urged.

"I'll be there, just be ready," he said, as he slid out of the booth and walked away.

He turned to look back at me and smiled one last time.

"And what was that all about?" one of the waitresses whispered in my ear.

"Absolutely nothing. He's an old friend from high school," I lied.

"Yeah, right," she said, as she winked at me.

My head began to spin. First of all, I didn't want anyone at work to find out I was gay. Second, I had never had someone like Richard pay so much attention to me. It was hard to believe someone so beautiful wasn't arrogant.

"I haven't done this in a long time," I said, as I watched Richard light a cigarette. "I'm not usually this much of a pushover."

"I've never picked someone up in a restaurant either. You are different than everyone else."

"Good different or bad different?"

"Good, of course. This was the hottest sex I've ever had." He reached over and stroked my leg.

"This your first time?" I joked.

I was shocked by his compliments.

"I'm twenty years old and I've had sex with several guys and with the exception of one other person, this was my best experience," I admitted.

He pushed his hair away from his face and took another drag on his cigarette.

"I'm sorry we had to do this cheesy hotel room thing. I live with my parents and there's no way we could have gone to their house."

"You don't have to apologize. I'm in the same situation. But if you keep rubbing my leg like that, you're going to have to pay the price of getting me started."

"I can afford it," he said, as he extinguished his cigarette and ran his hand further up my leg.

I spent my hours at work in extended daydreams. I lived and breathed for the moments that Richard and I were together. From February until April, I couldn't think about anything else. My job at Chi-Chi's became secondary, as did my plans to save money for my move to Los Angeles.

One Thursday, after work, I made a quick stop at the Wyoming Valley Mall to look for a new pair of shoes. The bus route went right by the hotel where Richard and I always met.

I noticed Richard's Trans Am in the parking lot. I knew he didn't live there and that was a day he said he couldn't meet because he was busy.

While I felt somewhat betrayed, I knew that we had never discussed exclusivity. I should have been the last one to be surprised. There were several times during our brief history that I had succumbed to the primal urge to do the same thing.

For a week, I couldn't bring myself to call him for a rendezvous. I knew he was probably wondering what had happened to me. I was struggling with the realization that although our sexual relationship was incredible, we shared nothing else. Whatever it was that we were having together, it wasn't enough.

Finally, on a Friday afternoon, I called him and we met at the hotel. After not seeing him for a week, I melted when I saw him. I told myself I could question the worthiness of the relationship after sex.

"I need to ask you a question," I said, as I pulled on my shirt.

"I'd prefer it if you'd ask me while you were naked," Richard encouraged.

"Would that fulfill some fantasy of yours?" I asked, once again caught up in the magic sparkling of his eternally blue eyes. He winked at me as I pulled off my shirt.

"Is what we're doing here enough for you? I mean, do you ever want more than just a roll in the hay?"

Richard's face became drawn and the liveliness left his eyes.

"Of course I do. Isn't that what everyone wants?"

"I think so. Do you ever want anything more from me? Is this capable of progressing beyond sex?"

Richard sat up and put on his T-shirt. Then, he just sat there in front of me. It was the sexiest thing I had ever seen. How could I want anything more from this guy than just sex? He was perfect.

He lit a cigarette and lay back on the bed.

"I'd love to take this to the next level."

Then his eyes grew cold.

"I could never build a personal relationship with you because I can't come out of the closet."

"What do you mean?"

"My family would disown me if they knew I was gay. I'd lose everything. I could never pursue a relationship with a guy for more than sex. Anything else takes too much time and I wouldn't be able to hide it."

"Are you sure your family would disown you?"

"They're Catholics. It would happen, believe me."

I sat on the bed next to him and brushed his hair away from his face.

"I understand. I don't think I could ever tell my family either. They're fundamentalist Christians. My father's a Baptist minister, for crying out loud!"

Richard laughed and drew again on his cigarette. "We're really fucked, aren't we?"

I nodded.

"Yes, we are."

We laid on the bed next to each for an hour, talking about ourselves and our lives. Richard's family owned one of the largest manufacturing companies in the state of Pennsylvania. He worked for them and even though he was twenty-two, he lived with his parents simply because the house was big enough.

Richard told me that if he ever came out to his family, they would cut him off. The money and the power that came with it was too much of an enticement to stay in the closet. I understood his predicament.

We also talked about me seeing his car at the hotel a week earlier. It was after that discussion that I began to realize how different we were. While Richard was flawless when it came to sex, he did lack some strengths that would have made me more interested in a deeper relationship.

I swallowed my fear and also brought up the subject of our safe sex. He responded to my concerns by physically reminding me of how stimulating it could be.

Our talk that day gave me a clearer perception of our relationship. It was just physical. There were no strings attached. That revelation provided some relief, but also rekindled the deep feeling of emptiness I had experienced my entire life.

When I left the hotel that day, I made a promise to myself that I would one day find the strength to come out to my family and everyone else I knew.

It was easy to become comfortable with the level of our relationship. I was able to resume pursuing my goal of moving on to Los Angeles.

I became quite professional at brushing aside the nagging feelings of loneliness and the traces of guilt. I just couldn't figure out if the guilt was from my ever present knowledge of the Bible, or if it was the smart side of my brain telling me that I should be investing my energy elsewhere.

16

It was odd to hear the telephone ringing at 11:30 at night. Richard never called that late. After two rings, I lifted the receiver. My mother had already answered it on their extension, and I could hear her conversing with a familiar voice.

"I think he's still awake. I'll go down and get him for you."

"I'm on the line, Mom," I broke in. "Thanks."

I heard the dull click as she hung up her end. There was silence for about two seconds.

"Marc, do you know who this is?"

My pulse began racing. I didn't want to know who it was, but Todd's voice was unmistakable.

"Yes, I do."

"How are you?" I asked.

"I'm fine. How are you?"

"I wanted to apologize."

"For what?"

There was a long silence.

"For not being a better friend to you. I'd like to get together and spend some time getting to know each other again. I miss your friendship. You were the one person who never let me down, and I'd like to have you back in my life."

I didn't know whether to hang up in disgust or promise him I'd be out on the next plane.

"I hope you understand this is a surprise to me. I never thought I'd hear from you again. You never called me after you visited me at Liberty."

"I know. I'm sorry about that. I understand if you don't want to see me. I just wanted to let you know that I'm sorry I didn't take better care of our friendship."

It was hard for me to tell if he was talking about a friendship or a relationship. I wasn't sure at that point how involved I wanted to get, if it was only going to be a friendship. Wasn't I going through that with Richard? I didn't know if I could only have a friendship with Todd.

"I want to see you. Would you like me to come and visit you? Where are you?"

"I'm in Florida. It probably wouldn't be a good idea to come here. I don't live too far from my parents and I don't want them involved. This is between you and me."

That was a different tune. Todd had never excluded his family from anything.

"I'm planning on traveling to Los Angeles in about a month," I said. "I'll be moving there in August and I wanted to get an apartment. Maybe we could go there together."

"That would be great! I've always wanted to go to California. It would be a great place for us to be away from anything that could cause problems."

Todd's enthusiasm was encouraging, but a warning bell keep ringing in my head when he talked about avoiding problems.

"I'll call and see if I can get another seat on the plane."

"Whatever you work out will be fine. I can take as much time off work as I need. This is going to be great!"

"Give me your telephone number and I'll call you tomorrow evening." I was trying not to get too anxious. The pain of previous disappointments was still vivid.

Twenty minutes later, I found myself unable to sleep from excitement. The prospect of seeing Todd again overwhelmed me. It had to be worth the chance.

I hadn't met another guy who was capable of making me feel the way he did. The strange thing about it was that even after all the time apart, just hearing his voice made me weak. What was it about him that could cause me to lose control? It had to be something much deeper than lust.

I couldn't wait to tell Carol the next day. I couldn't tell her exactly who Todd was, but I wanted to tell her about my confirmed trip to Los Angeles. I had to tell someone something or I would burst.

When I heard her boyfriend's car pull up in the driveway, I went into the living room and sat by the front door. I could hear them talking out on the porch.

"I can't wait to see you tomorrow," her boyfriend, Chris, said.

"I get off work at three," Carol replied.

There was silence for a long time and I had to force

myself to think of my worst nightmare to keep from visualizing them making out.

Chris finally broke the silence.

"I don't want you to talk to your brother anymore."

"Why can't I talk to him?"

"Just don't do it. You're my girlfriend now and I need you to listen me. Will you promise me that you won't talk to him anymore?"

"Sure."

Carol's response was hesitant and followed by silence. I knew they were back in their embrace. I slowly walked out of the living room and back to the kitchen. I couldn't believe that Chris would ask Carol not to speak to me.

It hurt even more to know that she had agreed to it. The whole thing seemed surreal. Carol's bond with Chris was very strong, I already knew that. I never imagined she'd sacrifice her relationship with me for him.

I focused my energy on my upcoming trip and the excitement I felt about seeing Todd. His effort to contact me was monumental compared to the lack of interest so many others were showing.

I couldn't share the excitement over the upcoming trip with Richard. I didn't want him to know that I was about to spend two weeks somewhere across the country with someone I once loved. One of the benefits of our sex-only relationship was that there was no accountability. In this instance, I was glad for it.

Our flights were arranged so that we met in Atlanta and flew the rest of the trip together out to LA.

We agreed to meet each other at the gate. My flight arrived in Atlanta about an hour before Todd's, so I had the privilege of a long layover.

Then suddenly, there he was, in a casual black suit with a white T-shirt. I was wearing a casual white suit with a black T-shirt. I leisurely shook his hand and made small talk as we boarded the plane and sat down. I hope he didn't notice that I was trembling. Then I noticed that his hands were shaking, too.

Once we were airborne, I relaxed a little. I could feel Todd's eyes staring at me.

"Do I look different then you remember?"

"Absolutely. You look older."

"Gee, thanks a lot. I'm still younger than you."

There it was. That damn smile.

"Do I look like the Todd you remember?"

"You look older, too. Maybe it's not so much older as it is more mature. We were nothing but a couple of kids, you know."

"I remember."

We spent the rest of the flight talking about everything that had gone on since we had last seen each other. For the past two years, Todd had been working as a staff artist for a major Florida retailer.

My tales of my final Liberty days and updating him on Debbie's state of affairs seemed to pale in comparison. He had been able to do what I had only just begun doing. It was inspiring to hear how he had reached some of his goals.

We carefully skated around discussing anything that had to do with our sexuality. However, during the flight, Todd kept his leg firmly planted against mine. It drove me crazy, but somehow I survived.

When we arrived at our hotel, I knew the sleeping arrangements would come into question. But when we got to the room, my concerns dissipated as Todd had requested a room with two beds.

After taking a shower, I sat on the corner of one of the beds and began flipping through a travel magazine left in a dresser drawer. Until he sat behind me on the bed, I hadn't even realized he was out of the shower. He tapped me on the shoulder.

"There's one thing we haven't talked about."

He was reading my mind.

"And what's that?"

I didn't turn around and look at him. I didn't want him to think this was too important.

"We haven't discussed whether or not we're going to have sex."

"I think I mentioned on the telephone that I didn't want to do anything."

"I just want to know if you still feel that way."

"I do."

I couldn't believe I was playing hard-to-get. It apparently wasn't a convincing performance. I felt Todd's legs straddle my body as his arms reached around in front of me. He pulled me close to him. I could feel his heart pounding hard against my back. He rested his chin on my shoulder.

"Is it okay if I do this?" he whispered, his voice breaking from emotion.

"Yes, it's okay," I managed to whisper.

I stood up and turned around and looked down at him. I knelt next to him. I stroked his face with my fingers, still not believing that we were together. He pulled my head towards his and kissed me.

In seconds, we were pulling off our clothes. I rolled over on top of him, touching him anywhere I could find skin.

"I have missed being with you," I whispered.

"I don't want to talk," Todd whispered back, pointing to his travel bag. "I've got condoms in there."

Around 5:00 a.m., I got up and went into the bathroom and turned on the light, gazing at my reflection in the mirror. Even though the sex with Richard and some of the other guys I had slept with had been very passionate, nothing equaled what I had experienced with Todd. It went beyond feeling a desire.

There was a meeting of our souls whenever Todd and I touched. It was what we had experienced together when we were at Liberty, and it was still happening almost four years later.

Instead of apprehensive teenagers, we were confident adults. No longer a guilt-ridden, uncontrollable urge, our sex was a harmonious expression.

Leaving the bathroom light on, I stood in the doorway and looked at Todd. He was sleeping naked outside the covers. I thought I had already had my time with Todd.

I felt like waking him up and telling him I loved him. I thought I had released him from my heart. Instead, I had buried the feelings because they had been too difficult to live with.

The moon shone into the hotel room and reflected off his skin, creating an almost surreal portrait of my lover. It was one of the most beautiful sights I had ever seen.

I knew then I was never going to be able to rid myself of my homosexuality. It was as much a part of me as the fact that I was my father's son.

The scars from years of struggling healed over almost instantly, and I finally felt peace. The peace I had searched for my whole life long came without effort.

"I am a gay man," I said out loud. I listened as the sound of my words disappeared into the darkness. I had never acknowledged who I was. My acceptance was my salvation.

I fell asleep that night without tears, worry or anxiety. It was a landmark experience, so personal and intimate, I couldn't have shared it with anyone.

The next three days of our trip were magical. Todd had a desire to visit the usual tourist traps. I was content just being with him. On Wednesday, halfway through our trip, I decided to throw all caution to the wind and make myself vulnerable.

We had just returned to our hotel from the Comedy Store on Sunset Boulevard. As Todd was showering, I was in the room mustering up courage.

"What are you waiting for?" he asked me, with a sly grin.

"I'm waiting for you to get your ass out of the shower so we can talk before collapsing from exhaustion."

"I'm sorry you hate doing all this tourist stuff."

I smiled and shook my head. "I enjoy being with you. Although, I never thought I'd have to visit every wax museum just to get laid. Come over here and rest your head on my chest."

Todd pulled the towel off from around his waist and did just that. He unbuttoned my shirt and put his hand inside. It was so comfortable to be close to him.

"I have something that I want to ask you," he said.

"Go ahead, and then I have something that I want to tell you."

There were a few moments of silence before Todd spoke again. "This trip with you has been one the greatest experiences of my life. Before I came out here, I had reached an all-time low. I was very lonely and I wondered if I would ever find someone I could really care about."

Silence again. I thought he might be crying but I wasn't sure. I just let the moment live.

"None of the relationships I've tried to establish have succeeded," he began again. "There has always been something missing. Until this week, I didn't think there was any hope. But now I've found you again."

He sat up on the bed and looked down into my eyes. He was crying.

"You are what's missing in my life. I love you, Marc. I want to be with you. I'd like to build a life together. I don't know when or how it will happen. I just know I want you with me for the rest of my life."

Todd ran his fingertips across my cheek and over my mouth. He ran them along my jaw and then rested his hand on the side of my neck.

"I don't want to wake up without you waking up with me," he continued. "I won't be happy unless I see your face every morning."

I smiled and wiped a tear off my cheek that had

dropped off his face.

"I have been trying to harness my feelings this entire trip," I said. "I love you, too. I have loved you since the day you first walked into my room at Liberty. Since the day you left my Aunt Lisa's house, I've been trying to fill the void you left behind. Yes, I think we could make a great life together. I never want..."

My words were cut off as Todd kissed me.

"I don't want you to say anything else," he whispered.

"I want to say that I love you," I said, holding his face in my hands and staring into his eyes.

"I love you, too. I promise on my life, that this time, I won't disappoint you."

All that was left to do was figure out how we could merge our lives. We made plans to go back to our respective homes, and then move to Los Angeles in January. The idea of a six month separation drove me crazy.

The next day we were off to Las Vegas for the final two days of our trip. The four and a half hour drive passed quickly, as we shared more with each other about the directions our lives had taken since we had last been together.

Todd was still interested in church and Christianity. But that was one of things about Todd that was so attractive. He consistently looked for the good things in every situation. Sometimes it was annoying, but most of the time it was refreshing.

On the way to Vegas, Todd wanted to stop in Pomona, to visit Dr. James Dobson's ministry facilities. We watched Dr. Dobson and his sidekick, Mike Trout, in action as they recorded a radio program.

I felt very uncomfortable, knowing how much hatred Dr. Dobson had for homosexuality. Todd was in heaven. He even made it a point to go by the personnel office to see if they needed anyone in the graphics department of their magazine.

"I can't believe you'd be interested in working for this place. Don't you know they'd fire you if they found out you were gay?"

"Maybe. I listen to Dr. Dobson's radio program every day at work. He seems like he's smarter than that."

"Dr. Dobson holds to the same ideals as any other Bible-believing Christian. Do you really think he'd go against what he reads in his Bible?"

"You're right, he probably wouldn't," Todd admitted.

Todd was uncomfortable talking about the subject of Christianity and its position on homosexuality. I hoped I could help him overcome it. Someday, when the time was right, I would talk to him about it again.

The Vegas trip went way too fast and soon we found ourselves back in Los Angeles packing our suitcases to return home the following day.

Suddenly, Todd sat on the bed and began to cry.

"What's wrong? What happened?" I asked, as I knelt down on the floor in front of him.

"I don't want to go back to Florida," he said, as tears ran down his cheeks. "My life there is awful compared to what I've had here with you. I just want to be with you. I wish I had enough money so we could just stay here."

I closed my eyes. He did feel the same way I felt. I knew I had to be the stronger person.

"I don't want to go back to Pennsylvania, either. I can't even think about how hard it is going to be to say good-bye to you tomorrow. I promise you that I'll love you in January as much as I love you today."

I reached up and held his face in my hands.

"It'll go by quickly," I lied. "Soon we'll be building a life together and this struggle we're facing tomorrow will be over. Then, we'll have the rest of our lives to dream together. It'll be okay. I promise."

We held each other for the rest of the night. I wanted to tell Todd that I would be more than happy to take the chance and never return to Pennsylvania.

Todd slept the entire flight from LA to Dallas/Ft. Worth. My brain was reeling from what had happened during just one week. Had I actually found the one? Or was it just a phase that would disintegrate with time?

I was madly in love with Todd, yet angry at myself for falling for him again. I couldn't find answers to any other questions I faced. Our plane arrived late, leaving us only a few minutes together before my connecting flight left for Washington/Dulles and Todd's flight left for Tampa.

"Well, this is it," I said.

I couldn't keep my voice from breaking.

"I don't want to leave you."

"We have to be strong," Todd encouraged.

"I know."

Boarding for my flight was announced as I stared into his eyes. I wished I could take a piece of him with me for comfort.

"I don't give a damn about what anyone thinks," I said, as I embraced him.

"I love you," I whispered in his ear.

I turned away and walked to my gate. I couldn't look back. I had to put myself in a trance to board that plane.

I awoke the next morning tired and disoriented. The birds singing merrily outside my window made me angry.   Fortunately, I had a day to recuperate before I started back to work.

My life alone in Pennsylvania was so dismal compared to what I had experienced with Todd. It was odd not having anyone around while I showered and got dressed. I had quickly gotten used to having Todd there in the morning. Something about his companionship was so soothing to my life.

I called Todd that night and he called me on Monday night. Our conversations lacked the openness we experienced when we were together. Inside, I was reeling from love sickness and I could hear the same illness in Todd's voice.

I stood around at Chi-Chi's on Tuesday trying to figure out how I could stop mourning and get on with my life. Going to California together had been a great decision. Deciding to live apart for six months had been a bad one. I knew it and I just hoped that Todd knew it, too.

If I wasn't living in my parent's house, I would have called him and asked him to come and live with me until January. I wanted to leave Pennsylvania and live with him in Florida until January.

Finally, late on Tuesday night, I picked up the

phone to call Todd and lay it all on the line. There was no tone when I picked up the receiver, and I was startled when I heard Todd's voice.

"Hello?"

"Hi, Todd, it's me. I just picked up the telephone to call you. It didn't ring or anything."

"I was calling you, too."

The openness was back. The walls we had built to protect ourselves were gone.

"I'm going nuts here, Marc. All I do all day long is think about you. I want you here."

I couldn't believe what I was hearing.

"You want me to come to Florida?"

"Yes, I do. This being apart until January business isn't going work. Will you move to Florida and live with me until January?"

"Of course I will. I need to take care of a few things, but I can probably be there on Thursday."

"I thought it would be easy to wait until January. When I got back here, I realized how much I want you to be a part of my life. Not in January, but right now."

"That's exactly what I've been going through. I was going to call you tonight and ask if I could move in with you until January. All I think about is you."

"I love you."

"I love you, too," I echoed. "Let me call the airline and then I'll call you back to let you know when I'll be there. Give me about fifteen minutes."

I walked into Chi-Chi's the next morning and resigned. It was uncomfortable and I knew that I disappointed my managers, but I didn't care. I was free. Just as I was about to end my shift, the hostess called back to the kitchen and told me that I had customer who requested one of my tables.

I knew it was Richard. There he was, sitting in the lobby of the restaurant as beautiful as ever.

"How are you?" I asked, trying to maintain control of my feelings.

"I'm fine," he replied, as he flashed me a beautiful smile.

Was he trying to kill me?

"I haven't heard from you in almost two weeks. I've got so much to tell you about."

"I know I'm sorry. I've been out of town. Can we go outside and talk?"

I waited to begin until Richard lit his cigarette.

"Just because I haven't called you doesn't mean I haven't thought about you," I said, slowly.

"I've missed you," he began.

He concentrated on every word he said.

"I missed everything about you. I thought a lot about some of the things we've talked about. You know, like if our relationship could ever go beyond just a sexual thing."

"We talked about that," I recalled. "You said that you could never tell your family that you were gay."

Richard nodded and looked at me. His eyes grew cloudy and despondent.

"I told them. I told my family I'm gay. I can't believe I did it, but I did."

I didn't expect Richard to tell me that.

"I decided that all of their money didn't mean shit to me if they didn't accept me. I did it because you were right. I do need more for my life than closet sex. I want to have a full-fledged relationship. I'd like to try to have that with you."

I closed my eyes. The airline tickets I had picked up on my way to work were burning a hole in my pocket. When I looked back at him, he was crying

"It's too late, isn't it?" he asked.

There was so much sadness in his eyes, I had to look away. But then I looked back.

"I've reunited with someone I knew in college. I'm leaving for Florida tomorrow to move in with him. His name is Todd."

The words sounded empty. I knew how they would sound to me if I was hearing them from someone else.

"It's great that you told your family. A relationship isn't worth having if it's not grounded in truth."

I didn't mean for my words to sound hollow and insincere. I wanted to comfort him. I wanted to wipe the tears off of his face and tell him how courageous I thought he was.

Richard tossed his cigarette onto the ground.

"I know" he admitted. "I wish it was you and me instead of you and some other guy."

"I'm sorry."

"Can I ask you one thing?"

"Anything."

"Would you like to have sex once more? It might make this easier for me. I never thought that the last time we were together would be the last time. I have my own place now."

I could vividly remember everything about him and our sexual relationship. The burning sensation I felt the first day I saw him returned.

I wanted to walk over to him and run my hands through his hair and touch every sensual spot on his body. I knew right where they were. I wanted to kiss him and taste the peerless passion I knew so well.

Richard's proposal was alluring, but I knew that I might feel differently if I slept with him in his new state of mind.

"I'm not going to lie—to you, Richard," I stammered, trying to keep my voice from shaking. "I won't pretend that I'm not captivated by you. I would like nothing better than to go to your place right now. But I made a promise to Todd that I wouldn't see anyone."

"He wouldn't know."

"You're right, he wouldn't. But I would."

"Fuck you," he said harshly.

Then he turned around and walked away.

I was stunned by the abrupt change in his emotions. No one had ever said that to me.

He had made a mighty sacrifice by telling his family he was gay. I knew he had done it just to be with me. I watched as he got into his Trans Am and peeled out of the parking lot.

I wept silently under my sunglasses as I rode the bus home that day. I knew that had I had sex with Richard, it would not have made him feel any better. And, it definitely would have confused me. Still, the separation hurt. I cared for Richard more than I was willing to admit.

It was hard to believe that I had enough restraint to turn down Richard. The promise I made to Todd was an important one for me to keep.

"I must really love you," I said aloud, looking at a photo from our trip that I kept in my wallet.

My parents agreed to drive me to the Philadelphia airport to catch my flight to Tampa. It was a long, silent ride. I wanted to tell them the truth about what I was doing. I had only told them that Todd was a friend from Liberty. I needed the ride to the airport, so I knew that the timing wasn't right to come out to them. They must have been thinking something, but they didn't ask any questions.

As the plane taxied to the runway, a burden lifted from my shoulders. My life in Pennsylvania had ended for good. This time there would be no coming back. So much had happened in my life since I had left for Liberty. No one could have told me that I would end up moving to Florida, and then to Los Angeles, with someone like Todd.

Actually, I never imagined I would be living with a man. The concept hadn't entered my mind four years earlier. I entered Liberty thinking that I would find a wife there.

The flight gave me time to think about my experiences at Liberty, the unstable relationships I had attempted to develop since I had moved back to Pennsylvania and the life that was waiting for me at the gate in Tampa.

I stepped off the plane and into Todd's embrace with a feeling of renewal. He was very self conscious about people around us, so I didn't cling to him like I wanted to do. We went to dinner from the airport. It was great to be with him again.

"It seems like we've been apart four years instead of just four days," I said, as we ate.

"I know," he agreed, never taking his eyes off mine.

"I can't believe that last week at this time we were committed to spending the next six months apart and now here we are. We're pathetic."

"I'm so excited that we get to do this now."

"You'll love my apartment."

"I'd live in a box, as long as we were together."

"Ah, you're waxing sentimental."

"Yes, I am. I'm lucky to be here with you."

"And I'm lucky to be here with you."

What might have sounded like romantic, insincere banter to the rest of the world, was music to our ears.

17

Whenever Todd and I would go out, even if it was just to the grocery store, I could sense tension.

Finally one night, after rushing out of a restaurant almost before I was finished eating, I opened the floodgate.

"What the hell was that all about?" I asked, as he started the car.

"There were some people in there that I didn't want to see. I also didn't want them to see you."

"I'm sorry but I'm a little confused. Are you running from someone or something?"

I stared out the window into the darkness, as Todd drove another mile or so in silence. Then he turned down a dirt road, pulled to the side and shut off the car.

"I should have told you about this. I haven't shared this with you because I needed some time to prepare myself."

"I'm here to listen, Todd," I offered.

"Okay."

Todd paused a few more moments and gripped the steering wheel tightly.

"Remember when you were here a couple years ago?"

"You mean when your mother threw me out?"

"Yes, then. Remember we took you to see Pastor Starlen before taking you to your aunt's house?"

"I remember. Go on."

"George Starlen was more than just my pastor. He was a good friend. I knew him several years before I even came to Liberty. He did important things for me. He knew my father didn't do squat for me. Instead of my father, it was George Starlen who would show up at my soccer games and go to my art shows. He was always there, supporting me."

"Well, that's a good thing. We all need someone to do that for us. God knows, I could have used someone like that in my life."

Todd turned and looked at me. There was fear or something like it in his eyes.

"Pastor Starlen was always trying to get me to do things with him. Sexual things."

"He was like sixty or something, wasn't he?"

"Yes. But I was a teenager. He was very affectionate. It was difficult for me to realize at first that he was doing something inappropriate. I needed a congratulatory hug after winning a game. It was the fact that he held me too long that made me feel strange."

"Later, after I quit Liberty, he became much less subtle in his approach. He must have become frustrated that I was not reciprocating."

I knew where the conversation was going.

"Well, what else would he do to you besides hold you too long?"

"We went to see a movie together once and he tried to feel me off."

"What?"

Todd sighed.

"We went to see some stupid movie and he tried to grab my crotch. I pushed his hand away and he didn't do anything else that night. On another occasion, he told me he wanted to give me a blow job. He frequently asked to borrow my gay magazines. He was always asking me if he could rub his head on my stomach."

"What the hell did that mean?"

"I don't know. I never let him do it. I never let him do anything to me. He kept trying, though. I also found out that he was molesting other boys in the church. Some of them were much younger than me. He even asked me how big your dick was."

"And you told him?"

"I didn't tell him anything."

"Why didn't you blow the whistle on this weirdo? He was taking advantage of his position just to get you in bed."

Todd nodded.

"I slowly realized what was going on. It was difficult because he had tricked me into needing his attention and affection. Whenever I would push him away, he would refuse to show up to my soccer games that week or he would do something to try and make me feel guilty. I needed his attention and affection. I would always break down and take him some of my magazines or something."

I understood Todd's neediness for someone to care about the things he was doing. I remembered all the nights I used to wish that my mother or father would take an interest in something I liked to do. I would have sacrificed just about anything to have their approval. That was a long time ago. I looked over at Todd and he looked at me.

"So what else happened?" I asked.

"Well, about six months ago, I was invited by Jerry Johnston to move to Kansas City and be a staff artist for his ministry."

"I remember him. He used to come to Liberty and hold revival services. In fact, he quit Liberty just so that he could work his ministry full-time. He always preached about kids on drugs and Satanism stuff. I remember one time when I was working in the public relations office at Liberty, I had to call his office to try and schedule him for a week's worth of services. He was too expensive for us to have him."

"Sounds like Jerry," Todd continued. "Anyway, I gave him a portrait I drew of him and he invited me to come to Kansas City and get an overview of his ministry. Marc, it was like a dream come true. I really admired his preaching and I thought it would be fantastic to be involved with him."

"So he flew you to Kansas City just to see if you would like working there?"

Todd smirked.

"Are you kidding me? I had to drive myself. When I got there, I went right to his mansion and he gave me directions to the motel where I would be staying. He did pay for the motel, though."

"Well, glory be."

"This really isn't funny. I noticed that he would do all sorts of strange things."

"Like what?"

I began to wonder what this story had to do with the George Starlen story.

"Well, after a revival service, he suggested we all go out for pizza. He just dug his hand into one of the collection plates and handed us money. Also, at his house, he pulled up a flower and said, 'Replant it. Anyone who works for me needs to be a team player.' He made me clean up his kid's bedrooms, too."

"I thought you were there to talk about your job."

"After being his personal slave for a week, he finally met with me and said that his ministry couldn't afford to buy any equipment for an art department. He told me I would have to raise five thousand dollars before he could add me to the staff."

This story was unbelievable. Typical, but still unbelievable.

"I went back to Florida and raised the money. I begged and pleaded with everyone I knew. I started sending Jerry the money as it came in. I gave thirty days notice at my job and I was ready to go."

"Did you live here?"

Todd shook his head.

"No. I forgot to tell you about that. I was rooming with Pastor Starlen's son, Robert."

"Is he gay?"

"Yes. But I never slept with him, even though it would have been easy since we lived together."

"Did he want to sleep with you?"

"Oh yeah. He would constantly parade around the house in his underwear. One time, I was watching television and he came in and started humping the floor in front of my chair. I got up and left the room."

"Why didn't you either give in or move out?"

"He wasn't very attractive to me and I couldn't move out because by the time it got to be unbearable, I was almost ready to move to Kansas City."

"I can understand that. I'm sorry you had to endure it."

"About three weeks before I was going to move to Kansas City, I heard about another young boy in the church whom Pastor Starlen was molesting. I decided that I couldn't stand by and let anyone else go through the same thing."

"So you blew the whistle."

"I blew the whistle. I got the deacon board of the church to come to a meeting. Robert even admitted that his father molested him and he agreed to stand with me and say it. After I told the deacon board that I was gay and what Pastor Starlen had done to me, Robert caved and backed out on giving his testimony."

"So it was just you and the deacon board."

"Yes. And most of them had known George Starlen for forty years. They called me a liar and said that I was just in trouble with my homosexuality and was looking for a scapegoat."

I shifted in the car seat so that I could see Todd better. "That doesn't make any sense."

"It didn't have to. I was told to shut up and not make any further allegations. However, I scared the living daylights out of Starlen and he resigned immediately. He left town and hid out at the orphanage for boys that he ran in the Virgin Islands. He returned a week later, after everyone in the church begged him to come back."

"So no one believed you."

"A few people did. They were too afraid to stand with me, though. Winter Haven is a small town. People hate anyone who stirs up trouble. They hate gay people, too. I bared my soul to them, Marc. I told them I was gay and they threw me out. I was trying to stop him from being able to ruin any more boys' lives."

The last sentence came out heavy with emotion. I wondered how Todd had been able to tell me this much without crying. I watched as several tears finally fell from his eyes.

"I'm sorry for what he did to you, Todd."

"I am so confused now about love and trust and all of that. I know I have difficulty being intimate with you because of what the bastard did to my mind."

"You know what?"

"What?"

"All you need to know right now is that I love you. I am here with you and I'll never, ever let anyone harm you again."

"I know," he said weeping. "Unfortunately, that doesn't make me feel too much better inside. I don't think there's a whole lot you can do to make me whole."

"Let me try at least. We have the rest of our lives together. In the past, you certainly have been a stronghold for me. Now I can return the favor."

"All right," Todd agreed. "Where was I? Oh yeah. After the Starlen thing blew up in my face and I was getting threatening telephone calls, I decided to call Jerry Johnston and see if I couldn't move there a little sooner. When I called his office, his secretary told me that he was out of the country for a few weeks. I called his house and spoke to his wife, Chris. She told me that Jerry was at the office and that he didn't want to talk to me."

"Why not?"

"He had received calls from several of the members of Northside Baptist Church who told him that I was gay and that I had tried to ruin their church by lying about Starlen. Chris then told me that I should never call his office or her house again. After her little speech she hung up on me."

"So he totally blew you off."

"Yep. He had his secretary lie for him. I did try to call his office again but she refused to put me through. And to make matters worse, they refused to return any of the donations my friends and family had made in order for me to start the art department. They took the money and shut me out. My dream was over. They had won and I lost big time."

"Todd, I don't see it as a loss. I would have walked away the minute he asked me to replant the flower."

"Yeah, but haven't you ever wanted something so bad you'd give anything for it?"

"Of course I have. I know what you're saying. I'm sorry they screwed you like that. It's a typical fundamentalist activity."

"So you see," Todd continued, "Sometimes when we're out, I see people, or I'm afraid we're going to run into people, from the church. I don't want any more bad experiences from this."

"I thought maybe you were embarrassed to be seen with me because people might think you're gay."

"I wouldn't be embarrassed if people thought that we were gay. I'm sure we're not fooling too many people."

I smiled.

"I'm sure we're not. Thank you for telling me this. I'd like nothing better than to pay personal visits to both George Starlen and Jerry Johnston. But you know, we probably wouldn't be together right now if you would have gone to work for Jerry Johnston. Just like we wouldn't have even met if it wasn't for Jerry Falwell's dream to have a Christian college."

"I know it all worked out for the best. It's still very painful."

"I certainly wasn't trying to minimize your feelings. I'm just so happy that we're together. We've waded through some nasty waters to get where we are today. There's a lot of things that could have kept us apart."

I was thinking about Richard. He had come to mind several times since I moved to Florida. I wondered how his life was going.

"I hope it gets easier from here on out," Todd said, hopefully.

I leaned over and kissed him on the cheek. He responded and turned and kissed me on the lips.

"Hi, Betty," I said quietly, as I extended my hand.

"Hi, Marc, I'd shake your hand but mine are full."

"Here, Mom, let me help you with that."

Todd took her ashtray and her carton of cigarettes and put them on the kitchen counter. It felt strange to be in Betty's house again.

"Does it feel strange to be here?" Betty asked, searching my eyes.

"Yes, it does. The last time I was here wasn't pleasant."

"Well, we can leave and go eat now, if you like. I certainly don't want to dredge up any bad feelings for you."

I forced a smile.

"Sounds good to me. I'm starving."

It was a much less dramatic reunion than I had pictured. The four years between us seemed like four days. I could tell that I was much different than I had been when I had been thrown out of that house. I wasn't so sure Betty was different.

I wanted her to have changed. Even though I had despised her for a long time, I wanted to feel the love and acceptance she had offered to me before she knew I had slept with her son.

Dinner was very casual and I let Todd and his mother do most of the talking. I was hoping for an apology but it never came. I tried to hide my disappointment from Todd, but it didn't work.

"I think you just have to give Mom a little time. The fact that I'm emerging from the closet is a lot for her to handle. You being here again is even harder."

I shook my head.

"I just wish we could have talked more about what happened. She just wanted to avoid it."

"Why don't you call and ask her to meet you for

breakfast some morning. You two can talk alone."

Another great idea from Todd Tuttle's brain. His gift for searching for a solution for every problem was often irritating, but this time it was right on the money.

"I'll never feel comfortable around her if I can't say all the things I need to say. I'll call her tomorrow and see if we can't set something up for later in the week."

Betty declined that week and the next. I tried once more to get her to meet me, but she always had something that kept her from making a commitment.

I decided not to let it affect me. Her acceptance wasn't necessary for me to feel complete. I wished Todd could see that her rejection of me as his lover, was a rejection of his choice of a mate.

Two weeks before our move to LA, I received a letter with Carol's name and return address on it. I had forgotten that she had married Chris in September. I knew what the letter would say before I even opened it. I read the letter aloud to Todd.

"Dear Marc," I began, "I wanted to send this letter to let you know that Chris joined the Marines and we will be moving to New Mexico for a couple of years. I also wanted to let you know that I am pregnant. The baby is due in May."

I looked up at Todd.

"Does she think I care?"

Todd shrugged his shoulders and motioned for me to keep reading.

"I have a suspicion that you are gay. Before Chris and I will allow you to see our baby, we need a letter from you stating that you are not gay. In addition , we need to hear that you are no longer living with Todd."

"Can you believe her?" I asked Todd.

"What makes her think you would want to see her damn kid, anyway?"

"I don't know," I said, as I began shredding the letter. "I don't want to read anymore of this garbage. This makes me feel like coming out to all of them. I should write a letter to everyone in my family and every friend I ever made at Liberty. I'm going to get similar reactions from all of them. I might as well get it over with."

Todd shook his head.

"That might be very hard for you to handle. I mean, everyone you know turning on you? How is that going to make you feel?"

"Bad. But delaying it isn't going to make them change their minds. They're always going to believe what they believe."

"Why don't you wait until after we move to LA? Then we'll be settled and I can help you. We've got so much going on in our lives right now. Remember, I've done this already—with most of the people in my family. It's not easy."

"I don't care what my parents think. They've never approved of anything else I've done."

I did care.

"But it will be different if they don't want to talk to you. Coming out changes everything. Don't you think that they know that we're not just friends?"

I knew Todd was right. I just didn't want to believe it. Carol's letter didn't hurt too much because she had rejected me months earlier. Losing the fragmented relationships I had with my family and the few friends I had from Liberty, would be too much to handle at that point. I would have to wait until I could do it slowly, with my own timing.

The next week, we held a yard sale to sell everything that wouldn't fit into Todd's car. The sale was supposed to last all day, but everything was gone by noon.

Three days later, with everything we owned packed in the car, and fifteen hundred dollars to our names, we hit the road. None of Todd's family was there to see us off. I understood then, what Todd had been trying to tell me about making sure that I was prepared to deal with the ramifications of coming out.

After living in LA for seven months, Betty told Todd she wanted to come and visit us. She was working on a book manuscript and needed time alone to complete it. I had mixed emotions about her visiting us, but with a few exceptions, I kept my mouth closed.

We made arrangements for Betty to rent a furnished studio apartment for a month. At that time, Todd was working as art director for a printing company and I was working on building our own design business. I would have to spend a lot of time with Betty, and I was not looking forward to it. I knew she was not comfortable with Todd's gayness and she definitely wasn't comfortable with me. My intuition was that she, and the rest of his family, felt that I was responsible for Todd's homosexuality.

From the moment Betty stepped off the plane, I knew that the month would pass slowly. She was still having difficulty accepting our relationship. She would also try to get at me by trying to get Todd to talk about his old boyfriends.

Nonetheless, I tried very hard to accommodate her and make sure that my feelings didn't surface. I didn't want animosity to ruin the moments that the three of us spent together.

Todd was convinced that Betty's problems stemmed from her bad relationship with Jerah. That sounded like an excuse to me. The truth was jumbled somewhere in between.

I thought that we should be honest with her and always let her know our feelings. After all, she was on our turf. She couldn't begin to understand Todd's life if he didn't explain it to her. Todd had never been as comfortable with himself as he was at that point.

Halfway through her visit, we showed up at her apartment to go out for the day. When we walked into her room, her suitcases were packed and sitting by the door.

"What's going on, Mom?"

"I'm going back to Florida. Jerah keeps calling. I just can't take all of this pressure."

She looked right at me when she said that last word and I knew my suspicions were right.

"I think you're having a difficult time accepting my relationship with Marc," Todd said quickly.

"What?"

"This is the first time that I've ever been myself around you and I think it's too much for you. I know you don't like the fact that I'm gay, but you're just going to have to live with it. You're my mother and I need you to accept me for who I really am and not for what you think I was, or who I should be."

"Todd, I don't have any difficulties accepting you. I came out here to see you, didn't I?"

"Betty, I think Todd is referring to some things that have happened since we've gotten together. I can't tell you how many times I've had to listen to Todd cry about the pain he has from his family rejecting him. He's trying to say that you have a communication problem. You're not always honest with your feelings."

Betty walked up to me.

"Communication problem? I'm not the person with the communication problem, you are!"

I looked at Todd in disbelief.

"I'm out of here."

I turned around and walked out the door. I walked across the parking lot and bypassed the car. At that point, I didn't feel like being around Betty or Todd. I had been pushed to the edge once again. I knew Betty couldn't accept Todd any more than my mother could accept me.

"Marc, wait!"

I turned around to see Todd running across the parking lot towards me. I stopped and waited for him to catch up to me.

"What?"

"Where are you going? Let's just go home."

"I don't think I want to go home. I don't want to be around you or your mother right now."

Todd closed his eyes.

"I told her that I was tired of how she treats you and that I wasn't go to speak to her again," he said, his voice breaking on the last two words.

"Why did you say that?'

"I'm sick of my family rejecting me and rejecting you. This was the last straw. I thought that Mom would be able to handle it, but obviously she can't. I chose you, though. I didn't choose to stand with her."

"Thanks for coming after me. I didn't think you would."

"Well, it's time that I put you first in my life."

"Do you think she'll really leave?"

"At this point I don't care. I don't think we can have a decent relationship with her until she learns to accept my homosexuality. She just needs to realize that this is who I am. And you are who I love."

Todd didn't talk to his mother that week or the next. I wondered if he would ever talk to her again. He was finishing the coming out process with her. He really wanted her to accept him and his decision to choose me as his lover. I admired his courage. I wasn't ready to do that yet.

I opened Debbie's letter. Several newspaper clippings slid out of the envelope and fell onto the floor. I picked them up and sat on the couch.

"Dear Marc and Todd," I read aloud to Todd, who was making dinner in the kitchen. "Here are all of the clippings that I could find. I've already told you just about everything that's in them but here's pictures. It's hard to believe that this has happened."

I put the letter down and unfolded one of the clippings. I stood and walked into the kitchen.

"This one's lovely," I said, showing it to Todd.

"Homeless man rapes male prostitutes," Todd read aloud. "Why are they saying that he was homeless?"

"Technically, he was homeless. Debbie had kicked him out the night before he did this."

"I can't believe that Wesley raped two guys at gun point," Todd said, shaking his head.

I started to laugh as I continued reading the article.

"Listen to this. 'Graham, known on the streets of Wilkes-Barre as Daddy Wes, was arrested Tuesday morning.' "

"Daddy Wes?" Todd exclaimed, trying not to laugh.

"This is too bizarre," I said, still laughing. "I never even knew there were male hookers in Wilkes-Barre."

"That explains why that guy offered you money that one time."

Todd was referring to an incident that happened when I was still in Pennsylvania. While I waited for the city bus to take me to Shavertown, a man offered me a large sum of money if I would let him give me a blow job.

"That guy was strange. I never saw anyone that looked like a hooker—male or female."

I walked back into the living room and picked up the other news clippings. I walked back into the kitchen.

"Here are the clippings about his trial and conviction. It says that the guys went right to the hospital after Wesley raped them. They had all of the evidence they needed. He got nine years. Poor Debbie."

"Poor Debbie? What about her kids? They have it hard enough in that cracker town."

"Yeah, I know. It's too sad for me to think about."

Debbie had just given birth to her third child, Nicole, a few weeks earlier. She lived on welfare because Wesley refused to work. Joy sent us pictures of the apartment where they were living. There were holes in the front door and rats. Joy said there was a constant stench of dried urine from the apartment next door.

I felt a little guilty.

Over the next six months, Todd and I temporarily moved our design business to Phoenix after winning several bids. It was easier to complete the work there because we could interact with the decision-makers.

Phoenix was hot and very family-oriented. It was definitely not a city where Todd and I would feel comfortable spending any more time than was required.

While we were there, we decided how we could impact Debbie and her kids' lives. Debbie hadn't made very many friends in Pennsylvania and after the ordeal with Wesley, we were certain that life for the children would be harder than ever. We asked her if she would be interested in moving to Phoenix to have a fresh start for herself and her children.

She accepted immediately, and so Todd and I got to work. Due to income requirements, we had to lease an apartment for her in our names. It was in a beautiful family complex located across the street from a brand new elementary school.

Debbie didn't have a car, so we made sure she could walk to the grocery store if she needed. There were several strip malls within walking distance, so she could seek employment and free herself from her welfare dependency.

Todd and I furnished the apartment completely. We purchased airline tickets for her, the kids and Joy to fly out. Joy came to help Debbie get settled. She stayed for two weeks and then went back to Pennsylvania.

It was truly a new beginning for Debbie and her

family. There was no history for her there. The only people who would know about Wesley would be the people she let know. Phoenix was more racially diverse than Wilkes-Barre, which allowed Wesley, Jr., Monica and Nicole more freedom.

A few months after getting her settled, we were finished with our projects and we headed back to LA. I felt that we had really made a difference for them. It felt good.

Throughout the entire process, Todd and I didn't receive any support from my parents. While we were capable of handling the project ourselves, it would have been nice to hear them say they were happy for Debbie. I couldn't believe that my parents could go for so long without changing.

A month after returning to LA, Todd decided that he was ready to try to work out things with his mother. A phone call from Jerah, saying she had divorced him, led Todd to believe that perhaps she had changed in other ways.

Todd wrote her a letter and invited her to come out to LA to see us. She accepted, and after an awkward phone call, the plans for her visit were solidified.

"Here, she comes, I can see her red hair," Todd said, as he bit his fingernails.

I stood to the side and watched Betty hug Todd. It was as if nothing had happened and no time had passed between them.

"Hi, Marc," Betty said, as she embraced me.

Two years later, she still smelled the same.

"Hi, Betty. Virginia Slims and Red, still?"

Betty laughed.

"Don't remind me. The last time I took such a long plane trip I could still smoke in the airport! I haven't had a cigarette in five hours! Get me outside!"

"Do we look different to you?" Todd asked, as we walked to the baggage claim area.

"You don't, but Marc does. He looks a little more mature."

"You mean bald," I injected.

"I didn't say that," she laughed.

Betty did act different. She hadn't hesitated to hug me when she got off of the plane. That was a significant difference. She also had a freedom about her that wasn't even there the very first time I met her.

"I can't believe you divorced Jerah," Todd said, as we sat down in our living room an hour later. "I never thought you would do that. I think it's great that you are on your own. You were always happier when you were working."

Let's cut to the chase, I thought.

"Did you ever think you would hear from Todd again?" I asked, trying to steer the conversation towards what I wanted to talk about.

"Um," Betty stammered and tears welled up in her eyes, "I guess I thought he would get in touch with me when he was ready."

"I think the timing was right," Todd said, looking at Betty.

"When I left, my relationship with Jerah was in such turmoil, I wasn't capable of having a relationship with anyone. You guys were together but were still getting comfortable with yourselves."

She was right about that. It was hard to admit, but

while we thought we had it all together, we were still growing. Todd hadn't even come to terms with his position on Christianity until a year after he stopped talking to Betty.

When we took Betty to the airport four days later, I actually felt as if the visit had been too short. There were still some kinks that needed to be worked out, but the changes in all of us shone brightly that weekend.

For Todd, it was a time of renewal in his relationship with Betty. For me, it was a time of hope. Perhaps one day soon, Betty and I could have the relationship I hoped we could have the day I first met her, eight years earlier.

18

We invited Joy to come to LA for Christmas in
1992. It was a small step I wanted to take to bring myself
closer to coming out to her and the rest of my family. In
the back of my mind, I knew that it couldn't be long
before something came up about Todd and me being gay.

I never thought that she would instigate the
conversation. But, as fate would have it, a week before
Thanksgiving we got the following letter:

"Dear Todd and Marc,
There's a rumor going around and I need to know if
it's true. I don't want to believe it's true and I will
believe whatever you tell me.
Are you guys gay?
I don't think it's true, but I wanted to ask you. If
you tell me you are, it won't change the way I feel
about either of you. I love you because you're my
brother, Marc. And Todd, you've become like a
second brother to me.
Please write your response.
Love, Joy."

The only part of the letter I saw was '...it won't change the way I feel about either of you...' I knew that the time was right for me to come out to her. If I came out to Joy, I would have to come out to the whole family.

Todd and I discussed in depth how to handle the situation and we agreed that I should call Joy and tell her that we were gay. I wanted to follow up the telephone call with a letter explaining what it meant to be gay, as well as what our relationship was all about.

I knew that Joy didn't know anything about homosexuality, except for what she had heard in church or seen on The Old Time Gospel Hour. There were no openly gay people in her circle of friends.

"Hi, Joy, it's Marc."

She was hesitant to answer, but finally managed.

"Hello, I asked if you would write a letter."

"I know you did, but I needed to talk to you about it over the telephone. We got your letter a couple days ago. I was not surprised to hear that you heard rumors. I will tell you that I am gay and Todd is my lover. I'm not embarrassed or ashamed of it. I know you don't know very many people who are gay, so I will answer any questions you may have."

"Actually, you're the first person I've ever known who is gay."

"Are you surprised?"

"No, I'm not surprised. Can I ask you something?"

"Sure, go ahead. I want to help you understand what my life is all about."

"If you died today, do you know for sure that you would go to Heaven?"

She was trying to make sure that I was a

Christian. She was using the question of questions to get me to respond. I knew the follow-up questions, so I decided to put an end to it.

"Joy, I was brought up in the same house you were. I went to the same church, the same Christian schools. I know all of the lines and I know all of the answers. This has nothing to do with spirituality."

"The Bible says something different."

"I know what the Bible says. The last thing that I want to do is fight about who is right and who is wrong. What I want to hear right now is that you still love me and don't think of me differently."

There was a long silence.

"I still do love you and I pray for you and Todd everyday. I want to come and visit still, but I need you guys to do something for me first."

"What?"

"I need you and Todd to take AIDS tests and show me the results before I get there."

I almost dropped the telephone.

"What the hell are you talking about?"

"Watch your mouth. It's a known fact that the AIDS virus can live outside the human body for up to ten days."

I shook my head to stay conscious.

"Joy, I don't know where you're getting your information, but you can't get AIDS because you touch someone who has it."

"I knew you would answer that way," she shot back. "How many gays, lesbians and druggies will have to die before you accept the fact that it's God's punishment for living a life of sin."

"Don't forget," I said, "That up until a short time ago, I believed the same lies you still hold in your heart as the truth. I don't want to argue with you."

"I don't want to argue either," she replied calmly.

"Good. Has anyone else in the family said anything to you about me?"

There was more silence.

"Only Debbie. I asked her last week if it would bother her if you were gay. She said she didn't care if you and Todd were gay as long as you guys don't do anything to her kids."

That was the final straw. My heart broke in half and I had to fight hard to keep from crying. I couldn't believe that after all we had done, Debbie would stoop to believe the same lies.

"You already know how Carol feels," she continued. "Mary's never mentioned it, and neither has Mom or Dad. So are you going to do it?"

"Do what?"

"Take the AIDS tests."

I almost hung up on her right then.

"Never. Your ignorance about AIDS is astounding. If you're so worried about getting it then why don't you ask Debbie or any of your other friends to get a test?"

"AIDS is a disease that only affects fags, dykes and druggies. I've already said that."

"I think you should apologize for the way you are treating me right now."

"You're the one who should be apologizing!" she retorted. "You should have told me before that you were having gay sex. I've been exposed to you many times."

Then tears finally came and I couldn't hold them

back. "Joy, until you can apologize for what you've just said, I think you should hang up and not talk to me. That way I can still love you."

"Come to Jesus, Marc," she pleaded. "He can take you from your sin and give you what you really need. Ask for his deliverance and Debbie won't have to worry about her kids anymore."

I gently placed the receiver in its cradle and walked away from the telephone. Todd came out from the guest bedroom where he had been listening on the extension.

"I am so sorry, Marc," he said.

I waved him off as I sat down on the stairs. He sat down next to me and put his arm across my shoulders. I wept into his shoulder for an hour. I knew I would be rejected, but no amount of preparation could have made Joy's words less crushing.

"Remember," Todd whispered, "We talked about this. It's their loss."

"It just hurts. I would never touch Debbie's children. We've done so much for her. I can't believe that she would say that. And I can't believe that Joy is so ignorant. I would never put her life at risk."

"You're preaching to the choir, sweetheart. I already know. You need to remember that you're going to go through this with your parents and your other sisters. You've got to be strong."

"You're right. It's just a little more difficult to actually go through with it."

It took me two days before I could pick up my pen and write the letters I knew I had to write to Mary and my parents. Carol and Debbie's letters would be different.

In my parent's letter, I asked them to call or write

back to me. I wanted to hear from both of them what they had to say. My mother had a way of trying to answer for both of them. It was the only time I had asked my father for anything in my entire life. I just wanted a letter or a phone call from him personally.

Of course, all I got back was a letter written by my mother and signed by her for both of them.

Effective immediately, the letter stated that Todd and I were not welcome to stay together in their home. Under no circumstances would we ever be able to stay overnight there. She gave us both the same Christian witness speech that Joy had given.

I had spent two hours writing seven page letters to each of them and in response I got a brief note card. I waited for two weeks to see if a letter or phone call from my father would follow.

Todd sat with me in the living room when I finally called them.

"Hello."

"Hi, Mom, it's me."

"Hi, honey. I was just about to call you."

My mother should have had that printed on a T-shirt.

"I wanted to call in response to the letter I got from you."

"Well, there's not much more to say. You know we have to follow what's in God's Word."

"I know how you feel. I'm sure that you and Joy have already talked and she's told you about what's happened between us."

"Yes, we did talk. You can't blame her for wanting to be careful."

"Careful? I didn't ask her to have sex with me! We asked her to come and visit."

"She would just feel more comfortable if you were able to show her that you didn't have AIDS, yet."

Yet?

"Mom, how do you think people get AIDS?"

"Honey, everyone knows that AIDS is a germ that is created when two men have sex. God never intended for men to have sex with each other. This is his way of letting us know he's not happy."

I couldn't believe that my mother worked in hospitals for fifteen years and still thought that disease was a spiritual issue.

"I think you need to go to the library and get some information about AIDS. You're wrong about how someone gets sick. It has nothing to do with God. And it has nothing to do with men having sex. Anyone can get AIDS. It doesn't matter if they are male or female."

"I don't know about that. All I can go by is what God's Word says."

"The Bible doesn't say anything about AIDS."

"Do we have to talk about this now?"

"I guess we don't have to talk about this at all. I'm just disappointed that the first time in my life that I open up to you and Dad, I get treated like this. Do you know how hard it was for me to write those letters?"

"I don't know, but your father and I want you to know that we are concerned for you."

"Yeah, right. He didn't even answer my letter."

"You should know that he agrees with everything that I put in my letter."

"I just can't believe that he wouldn't take the time

to write back to me. I haven't heard anything from Mary."

There was silence for a few moments.

"She probably doesn't have anything different to say than Joy or Carol. They all have their own concerns."

"Yeah, I've already heard Debbie's," I snapped.

"You can't fault her for looking out for her children's welfare."

I couldn't believe I was hearing it again! "I'm sorry that you feel that way," I said quickly.

"It's not how I feel. It's how Jesus feels."

"Good-bye, Mom," I said quietly, as I hung up the phone.

Todd walked over and put his arm around my shoulders. This time I didn't feel like crying. I was too angry. I was angry at the people who had filled my family's heads with lies.

"I can't believe that they're all so ignorant."

"You did well. I only heard half of the conversation, but you handled it well."

"That's the last time I'll ever talk to her."

"I know."

"My own mother believes that I'm a health hazard and a pedophile. How can I reason with someone like that?"

Todd shook his head.

"You can't. You were right to end the conversation when you did. She'll die for her beliefs. A short time ago, we would have done the same thing."

I looked up at Todd and smiled.

"Don't remind me."

A week later, I got a letter in the mail with my father's handwriting on the envelope. Todd wasn't home from work yet, so I sat on our bed and opened it.

"Dear Son," I read aloud, "I hope this letter finds you well. I wanted to take a few minutes to respond to the letter you sent to me recently.

"As you know, I cannot condone your lifestyle, or as you call it, your sexual orientation. The Bible condemns this sin and we both know that the Lord will judge justly in this matter. I have no choice but to turn you over to the Lord for his judgment."

I let the letter slip from my hands and it slowly fell to the floor. I had read the words I needed to read. I was surprised that my father's words didn't make me angry. If anything, I felt relieved. I wasn't looking for a reason not to talk to him. God knows I had hundreds of those. I was looking to see if my father would choose to judge me instead of try to understand me.

No longer a preacher; no longer the preacher's son.

These Chains

I can remember the day
when someone first told me
what I felt in my heart should be gone.
I remember the embarrassment,
the grief and the wondering
as I questioned why God made me wrong.

I wonder if they know what they stole from me
How they robbed me of the joy of my youth.
They forced me to wander in a dark place
full of pain that could not be soothed.

I finally found my way back to life
as I learned what it means to be gay.
Whenever I feel those chains on my soul
I break them and throw them away.

MARC ADAMS - 1996